Yermiyahu Ahron Taub

The Education of a Daffodil

Yermiyahu Ahron Taub

The Education of a Daffodil

Prose Poems

Hakodesh Press

Imprint

Any brand names and product names mentioned in this book are subject to trademark, brand or patent protection and are trademarks or registered trademarks of their respective holders. The use of brand names, product names, common names, trade names, product descriptions etc. even without a particular marking in this work is in no way to be construed to mean that such names may be regarded as unrestricted in respect of trademark and brand protection legislation and could thus be used by anyone.

Cover image: www.ingimage.com

Publisher:
Hakodesh Press
is a trademark of
International Book Market Service Ltd., member of OmniScriptum Publishing Group
17 Meldrum Street, Beau Bassin 71504, Mauritius

Printed at: see last page
ISBN: 978-3-639-79497-7

Advance Praise for *The Education of a Daffodil*

Although he's a prose poet, Yermiyahu Ahron Taub's poems in *The Education of a Daffodil* demonstrate that he is also part storyteller and part playwright from another time. Somehow Taub weaves these genres together to create striking narrative tales of trauma, loss, displacement, sexuality, and xenophobia. Imagine a Yiddish bard from centuries past who creates scenes that mark his place in this post-modern world: that is Yermiyahu Ahron Taub. This courageous collection, which offers flickers of Lucille Clifton and flashes of Marge Piercy, won't let us forget that the past flourishes in the present, and that the unexamined life is a terrible waste.

— Carmen Calatayud, author of *In the Company of Spirits*

A gifted story-teller, Yermiyahu Ahron Taub inhabits many worlds: the world of the outsider, seeking connection, the immigrant, the yeshiva student, the fragile daffodil, the one who is bullied for being different, for being gay, the lover. This powerful book is his "extended sojourn into a labyrinth of pain and recovery." Through this foray into ballads, fairy tales, and parables, Taub gives us access to the journey of his own healing. This brave and brilliant book is a gateway to transformation, in which the reader feels like a confidante, a treasured and trusted friend.

— Deborah Leipziger, author of *Flower Map* and co-founder of *Soul-Lit*, a journal of spiritual poetry

In *The Education of a Daffodil*, Yermiyahu Ahron Taub offers his readers a sober, beautiful, and wild human choir. These delicate and powerful poems sing of women waiting for bombs to fall, aunts in kitchens, black veils. We hear of revolutionary lovers, alley kisses, an elderly woman who used to ride buses. We see a hero dance on a football field at night. We listen as he muses over the names the world has called him, the colors of his clothes. In this lush human chorus, we not only see the cruelties that land on some of us, we also see survival. It can be no surprise that this survival beautifully comes to us in poems. This collection of poems sings of survival. It's a song we all need.

— Joseph Ross, author of *Ache*, *Gospel of Dust*, and *Meeting Bone Man*

In *The Education of a Daffodil*, Taub carefully studies the singular experience of the *shlimazl* (a person who suffers through no fault of their own), a both fragile and resilient character who faces an estrangement from himself and others, and the essential foreignness of being human. Driven by a natural gift for storytelling, Taub's creative and meticulous prose poems find similarities between orphaned girls, an aging dowager never brilliantly beautiful, and the Orthodox Jewish boy dancing to the beat of a band in the shadow of a football stadium. With precision and a understanding for the layers and shades of human suffering, Taub captures what happens to the person who inherits "eyes ringed red from years of not looking away." For me, *The Education of a Daffodil* reads like a personal midrash on a single person's life. In an elegant and highly-tuned style, Taub retells the story of the underdog, bestowing upon this suffering figure the laurels of compassion, thus re-imagining him as a hero in his own tale, one in which he can say, ultimately, *I lived, I survived.*

— Leslie Contreras Schwartz, author of *Fuego*

In *The Education of a Daffodil*, Yermiyahu Ahron Taub charts a young man's journey from innocence to experience across a treacherous, sometimes painful landscape. These are meditative poems that look outward to characters both historical and contemporary, as well as inward to the dark corners of the heart. In poems that are by turns fearsome and ominous, tender and humorous, Taub takes between his fingers the "texture of experience," showing how we hurt and, ultimately, how we heal. There is danger here, violence and its aftershocks, but also a celebration of survival. This poet has "stardust scattered / throughout his song."

— Matthew Thorburn, author of *Dear Almost*

The Education of a Daffodil

Prose Poems

Yermiyahu Ahron Taub

די בילדונג פֿון אַ געלן נאַרציס

פּראָזעלידער

ירמיהו אַהרן טאַוב

2017

To survivors

and

to their beacons

Contents

II. LIFE STUDIES IN YELLOW (AND OTHER PRIMARY COLORS)

Before Art, History: After Repression, Art

In 2009, I began to experience recurring waves of fiery tingling in my hands and up my arms. I made appointments with an ergonomic specialist who realigned my computer keyboard and made other adjustments to my work station. I scheduled numerous appointments with neurologists, physical therapists, and other medical professionals. A variety of tests and procedures were undertaken. However, several nerve conduction studies revealed a normal nerve response rate. MRIs similarly produced no new insights into this phenomenon. Physical therapy provided some alleviation of the symptoms, but only for a short while. Splints were recommended for my arms both at work and during sleep. Topical creams to be applied at the wrists and hands were also prescribed. But none of these worked. My doctors were mystified by the persistence of symptoms without any discernible underlying cause. After more than three years of medical attention, I had only some added knowledge of human anatomy and physiology and a mounting sense of desperation to show for my travails. The spectre of carpal tunnel surgery hovered ubiquitously, offering the possibilities of redemption or lingering (or escalating) pain and wrist scar tissue.

A chance mention of my condition to a colleague transformed my life path. Through her recommendation, I landed in the clinic of Phil Tavolacci and TAVO Total Health. There, I was exposed to the process of myo-fascial release, and through Phil, to a broader naturopathic healing network. Eventually, it was suggested that I read the work of John E. Sarno, whose groundbreaking work on psychosomatic pain remains controversial within some medical circles. Sarno's discoveries on the uses of pain by the unsconscious mind to deflect and distract from deep-seated trauma and repressed rage proved invaluable to me as both a patient/client and artist. Through guided excavation, I explored a long-buried history of trauma, a process I've dreaded (and in some ways, still do) but which my body was demanding. The carpal tunnel syndrome symptoms abated immediately and entirely. But alas pain returned more than two years later, although in different parts of the body. The symptoms and the tenacity of the unconscious proved enduring. The process of healing proved to be more fragmentary, as the dread of engaging the legacy of darkness persist/s/ed.

The prose poems in this book, most of which explore dislocation and/or violence and their aftereffects, are consequences of my extended sojourn in this labyrinth of pain and recovery. Arguably, they are the logical next step on a path of coming-to-terms. They aim to investigate the texture of experience rendered visible after years of near total burial. The poems were crafted as narrative, sometimes drawing upon but not limited to personal experience and shaped by embellishment and fabrication. Of course, some are more directly autobiographical than others; I leave that determination up to readers.

However brief, this introduction was in some ways, the most challenging portion of this book to write and, in fact, was written (and included here) only after considerable deliberation and intermittent mortification. Poetry, even of the confessional (and prose-y) sort, thrives on the mysterious. Would I be stepping over a line that would become visible only in retrospect? Why risk upsetting the poetic equilibrium with such stark clinical revelations? Additionally, "coming out" about trauma in prose removes the veil of mystery afforded by poetry, even accessible narrative prose poetry. This introduction eliminated the possibility of a hiding place. I had to ask myself repeatedly: Am I really doing this? Am I really going to expose myself in this way? To what end? Furthermore, I did not want to risk placing art (too) squarely in the realm of therapy or postulating a direct causality between art and healing.

Despite these reservations, this introduction remains. On sum balance, I felt that the context enhances, rather than diminishes, the impact of the poems. Understanding the impetus of the poems is not the same as providing a justification for them. Far from positing causality between art and healing or even art as a shining exemplar of healing practice, I hope that this framework suggests an interplay of art and renewal that is more intangible, but no less rewarding. Vital even. I hope further that these disclosures will enlighten readers and enrich the overall experience of this book.

Yermiyahu Ahron Taub

∼ I ∼

BRIEF HISTORIES OF FEAR

In a Coach Without Chaperone

If Aunt Lavinia were in this coach, my ear would not be so elsewhere.
I could absorb the clop-clop of hooves and the clatter
of wheels over cobblestones and dust.
I could savor the sun eluding the velvet of these coach curtains
warming me well, despite the chill of the season.
All the while, I would absorb Aunt Lavinia's comments
on the conditions of boulevards and byways.
I would follow her diagnosis of the aforementioned curtains
and their effectiveness in preventing the sun from damaging
my priceless porcelain skin and her self-debate as to whether she should
tell the driver to stop so she could fetch that extra blanket from the trunk,
which she had insisted on leaving in said trunk at the journey's outset.

If Aunt Lavinia were in this coach, my hands would not be so atremble.
I would reach into my bag with purpose and remove the embroidery on
which I have been working and for which I have been so assiduously
trained. Here a sprig of violets for the center; just beyond, a fern border.
Pleasing would be this design for a parlor or a solarium of a sort.
I would focus on the movement of needle and thread through cloth and
enter the state of awareness and vacancy that embroidery can engender.
I would compose the invitation list of an informal soiree,
with she as hostess. I would transcribe the menus as Aunt Lavinia
balanced her guests' dietary needs with those demanded by the occasion.
Aunt Lavinia always appreciated my knowledge of the county
and the steadiness and clarity of my hand.

If Aunt Lavinia were in this coach, my eyes would not be so red.
For you see, not only is Aunt Lavinia not in this coach,
she is not with us at all.

Aunt Lavinia passed just a few weeks past.
I sat by her bedside with wet cloth; there was little that could be done,
despite the cameo appearances of the local doctor. He said it was
good that she went fast, given the ferocity of her agony. But it was not
good for Aunt Lavinia who had so much more to orchestrate and organize
and command and advise. She fought the the disease ravaging her
and cursed the march of its plunder and devastation.
And Aunt Lavinia who was all I had left in the world, who embraced me
when others advised her to expel me to the orphanage, is now gone.

If Aunt Lavinia were in this coach, my heart would not be so aflutter.
For if Aunt Lavinia were alive, I would not be in this coach at all. For all
her organizational savvy, Aunt Lavinia's last will was not impeccable.
Far from it. Distant relatives—cousins thrice removed—questioned
her state of mind, emphasized the sex of writer and beneficiary, and
snatched away all that was to be mine. If not for the kindness of one of
Aunt Lavinia's allies, my fate might have been far worse. However,
she remembered, that in addition to my embroidery and penmanship, my
skill with French went beyond the present and past tenses, and thus this
position to which I am now en route, was found. If Aunt Lavinia were
here, she would nod sagely at life's unpredictability and smile, and I
would not be so afraid of the widower and his brood awaiting me at
journey's end.

Orphan's Dowry

I bring you these arts of the kitchen gleaned from my mother,
her voice awhisper in the pantry, scanning, harvesting components, at
grace over the sink, shoulders back, chest forward, stirring the cauldron,
tendrils escaped from her kerchief, perspiration beading her forehead,
"Observe the caper of bubbles, the mood of the flame.
Fear not the fire. Now is the time for cumin; in a moment, saffron.
Follow the compass granted you by this feast unfolding."

I bring you these arts of the needle gleaned from my nana,
her eyes rheumy, ringed with red from years of not looking away,
huddled over fabric pierced, arranged without pattern, pins posted,
lines stitched so steady by fingers somehow still so sure,
a medley of whirring, humming, punctured by sighs, until finally,
a sky blue and white gingham frock ready for the picnic:
"There you are, my dear."

I bring you these arts of dance gleaned from my sister,
her voice skipping in the dark, her fingers gently prodding,
a kerosene lamp suddenly aglow, her hand around my waist,
my hand on her shoulder, whirling me through flickering light,
madcap shadows, guiding me towards nimble, my feet, my body
suddenly coming into knowledge: so this is how it's done.
"Yes," she answered, "Just so. This joy is now available to you."

I bring you these arts for they cannot be unlearned, despite the theft of my
mother seized from us so soon, her sweat no longer benign, despite my
protestation, despite Nana's disbelief for it surely could not be so, it surely
could not be so, despite my sister's flight from the abyss of her new role
with *better to go, better to just go.* And so my words are no longer to be
spoken, my eyes are no longer to be raised, my smile is no longer … to be.
But here are these loves. Here, savior, have these arts instead.

Concerts by the Sea

The day for Ada began like many another.
Mother prepared a breakfast of eggs and croissants with jam,
and they broke bread together without conversation,
as was their preference,
in the translucence of post-dawn,
punctured only by bird call and insect traffic and mastication.
Afterwards, Mother handed Ada a scrap of paper on which was written
the name and address of her new teacher. Ada was surprised,
for this was the first she had learned of Mlle. Sophie's departure,
which had occurred due to circumstances whispered of
in the millinery and other shops and even in the village square
but which could not be told to Ada during or after breakfast on that day.

And thus did Ada's day change,
and alas Ada had never been keen on change.
But following her mother's direction did Ada walk down the lane,
turning left under the canopy of the gnarled ash tree,
and take extra care with her violin, for her hands did shake so.
For Ada had thrived under Mlle. Sophie's instruction,
so precise and expansive, and Ada wished at least to have bid her adieu,
to have thanked Mlle. Sophie and wished her godspeed and good.
And Ada did walk up a path,
surrounded on either side by wild grasses and flowers,
to a cottage atilt with slate roof tiles missing,
and she was reminded of certain fairy tales from her childhood.

And Ada did not even have a chance to knock, but was greeted by
a man of late-middle years, who with pursed lips, informed her
of her tardiness by two minutes,
a most inauspicious beginning, young lady, he did say and
direct her to sit on a bench designated for pupils
surely possessed of a hardier constitution than Ada.
And then Ada did commence her playing.
She who captivated kinfolk and villagers alike
elicited a grimace and a command to begin anew from her teacher.
And Ada did comply,

but to the grimace were added a shaking of the head
and criticism torrential regarding all aspects of Ada's technique.

And thus did Ada depart the cottage of the teacher,
who did not attempt to persuade her to stay nor invite her to come again,
and thus did she return to Mother, who sat with her
and offered words of solace and sense,
even though Mother had marketing and other errands then to complete.
And Ada was grateful for such words as she sat with her mother,
and then as she placed her violin, purchased at such great cost,
in her bedroom closet. And although Ada was invited to perform
in the village and beyond, she declined all such invitations.
And although she did attend concerts, every fiber of her attuned to each
note and curlicue, Ada never did introduce herself to the artists
or advance her own standing in any way.

For Ada put aside the public, and did help her mother
in the house and in the garden and on the land so pitiless,
for there was much work to be done
and few hours in which to complete it. And although Mother
was disappointed in Ada's withdrawal from the public,
having encouraged her since little girlhood,
she took heart in her industry and dedication at home,
especially now that she herself was getting on and subject to ailments
not easily remedied by the herbs she gathered from field and forest.
Only Mother did not know the destination of Ada's afternoon walks,
or that Ada had transfered her violin from her bedroom closet
to a secret shelter by the sea from which she did remove it with care

and did resume play in the sands and reeds and dunes. There, in the light
that was the blue and slate of seaside, she recited the works
of the old masters and those of new ones, too.
And Ada did not, in fact, perform to an empty house.
For the creatures of the water, chiefly sea lions, came to listen.
And they proved most dedicated to her art, their barks
and other utterances sounding approval at the right moments.
And they did have their favorite composers, of course,
who shall not be spoken of here, and Ada did indulge them,
but also did return to those in less high a favor, for Ada always did

encourage the creatures of the sea to keep an open mind, as she had been
taught to do by Mlle. Sophie who had had to depart so abruptly.

And thus did Ada return the violin to its shelter by evensong,
and fins and tails awhirl, did the lions and other creatures return to sea.
And Ada did return to the home that was her mother's and hers,
sometimes with a few seashells whose scallop and color caught her eye,
sometimes with blooms or berries gleaned along the path.
And there she did peel the vegetables and scale the fish
and light the fire and there did they end their day with an evening
meal, together-bookends to their day of apartness.
And thus was the day that had heralded such change, from which
her Mother and the villagers said she had yet to be mended,
put into perpective of sorts. And thus did Ada, with music of the
masters and the sea creatures within, return to the opacity of night.

Clarissa's Convocation of Muses

There is no particular time of day.
She cannot depend on the signs of visitors approaching: the crunch of
wagon wheels on gravel, the rustle of muslin at May dusk. Even as she
scours floors and makes beds as instructed by her grandmother—
sides out, pillows above quilt, top of quilt folded under pillows—
even as she stocks the larder with goods from the general store
and frets over her ballooning debt there,
Clarissa knows she cannot will their arrival.

There are no particular tools.
She cannot shuffle, fan, or read cards with any dexterity. The Ouija board
has only ever remained still in her presence, despite candles flickering and
faces expectant all around. A crystal ball gathers dust in the parlor,
occasionally remarked upon by visiting spiritualists of various sorts.
Once she hung beaded curtains in doorways;
once she had a penchant for ornately flowered shawls. Once.
As fond as Clarissa is of these instruments, they ignore her beckoning.

There is no question of instruction.
Clarissa has no inclination to circles, where words artfully arranged are
dissected. Even if time could be found, even if she could sneak away
from meals and cleaning and duty, she would chafe under the
suggestions, however discreet. Nor do opportunities arise for grander
venues. For all their genteel revolutionary fervor, the salons, with their
damask divans and tinkling laughter, remain closed to her.
She is neither unaware of their charms nor surprised at her lack of access.

For Clarissa hears voices. Rather, voices find Clarissa.
Perhaps the baby Tobias has quieted; perhaps he is in mid-wail. Perhaps
Maude has just arrived with the latest gossip. No matter. Clarissa finds
a path into quiet. She stares at the blues of the worn carpet gifted by
Gran. She hears the rustling of apple trees, transfixed by the path of
blossoms drifting onto a naked bisque doll abandoned in mud. Clarissa
feels herself opening as word music drifts from her fingertips onto paper.
Maude shakes her head in disapproval; Tobias gurgles in wonder.

Dialogues in Transit

I. On the Bus to Charlottesville

A.

That chile sho' be loud; listen to 'im natter on.
Now he takin' to howlin'; I don' like the sound of it,
the way his breath catch at the end of each wail. Kinda wheeze like.
Umm. Umm. You feel me?
Why she gotta slap him like that? In the middle of his carryin' on, too.
It ain't right. I've a min' to call Child Welfare.
Beside, I need to get me some sleep on this here bus.
That damn dog at Mattie's kept me up all night. Crazy yappin'.
If it ain't one thing, it another; ain't that what I was jus' tellin'
Mattie last night? Puttin' up with Miz Lizzie's younguns all these years;
it my time for a lil peace.

B.

Why can't he be like other kids?
Why does he question, fight me at every turn?
I told him he couldn't have a snack just now;
he had one twenty minutes ago. I told him.
Good thing the licorice twists and Skittles were on sale.
Don't know what I would have done if they weren't.
He'd best stop that howling; he can't fool me.
Crocodile tears if I ever did see any.
Good thing there's hardly anyone on this bus;
I can't take this anymore either …
and he's mine!

II. At the Charlottesville Station and on the Bus to Lynchburg
   and Points South and West

A.

My goodness. Look at that chile go. Round and round.
I swear I ain't never seen nothin' like it. Wanda, you jus' gotta see this!
He runnin' up and down the whole station, now round and round.

She got him jacked up on speed or somethin'.
Don' she got some books for him? Some toys?
She could get somethin' at the Good Will. This boy he jus' bored. Lord,
I sho' hope they don' get on the transfer bus. Wanda, don' you know it,
thas exactly what they fixin' to do. This bus is crowded. I'm gonna
put my things down nex' to me, make sho' they don' sit here.
Oh good, here's a nice young lady comin' on; I'll move them for her.
Good Lord, Wanda, it sho gonna be a long ride to Nashville.

B.

Good thing he's getting to blow off some steam in this bus station.
Did I ever run like that? Unlikely. Mama wouldn't have let me.
If things were different, I could ask her. If I hadn't run away with Jamal
and produced this here "blue-eyed child of dusk come of no good, come
to no good" (her words, I swear), then … Well, then, I wouldn't have
had those years with Jamal, good and bad, until lately mostly bad with his
breath stinking of booze and his fists floating freely. I think I heard
someone once say that on Oprah. And I wouldn't be on this bus. *Will
someone please give us a seat?* Just one. I'm going back to where
it all started. Will Mama take me back? I swear I'll go to services
this time. Bobby, give your Mama some sugar. Baby, you're all I've got.

Musings (Made-Up) of Melanie

*(after the portrait, "Melanie, the Schoolteacher" by Chaim Soutine
at the Columbus Museum of Art, Columbus, Ohio)*

His reputation precedes him.
They say he walked on foot to the City of Light
from a town in the remote regions of the East,
where he was punished for violating the prohibition on the graven image.
And that his paintings are composed of brushstrokes of rage.
Even his trees are said to bear malevolence, or perhaps bear witness to it.
I wouldn't know; I haven't seen them. I'm merely stating what I've heard.
They say too that he lives a life of poverty,
which seems only to expand his ego and strengthen his determination.
Perhaps he'll find a patron undeterred, or compelled even, by rage and
focus. Some are so drawn. So perhaps.

Alas I am not of that persuasion. My father raised me to appreciate
all that was fine and good and restrained. He valued carefully hewn lines,
such as those to be found in the essays of X and the polemics of W.
He instilled in me the principles of frugality, of living simply if zestfully,
of discovering joy in the everyday—the black of coffee against white
porcelain under a breakfast sun, the rigors of an evening constitutional
through parks and along river banks and the pleasure of returning home,
taking the lift, or taking the stairs when the lift was out of order.
All of which drove my mother to mild (and then not so) distraction
until she left us altogether for charms more roiling, perhaps not unlike
those of this painter bent now over my unfolding likeness.

And thus I was left with the care of Father in the evenings, although there
was always a sharing of duties along expected lines, of course. I learned
to make crêpes and soufflés as he required, and he found the most
suitable wines for every occasion and quizzed me on my
Greek and and Latin and Hebrew. And when I received my
first-class certificate and was thus qualified to teach, he beamed so.
I had never seen such brightness on him in the muteness of our quarters.
And Father always had suggestions for me, for my students, recalling
what had succeeded for him, warming to his theme of how learning,

methodically attained, thoughtfully applied, cannot fail us.
There can be no shortcuts to Wissenschaft, Father insisted.

And here I am on canvas, at last, flattered to sit,
although doubting whether Father, gone these many years,
would have approved. *Vanity, chimera*, I can hear him say now.
Still, a form of immortalization. Hmm.
What of me has been visible to this painter?
My high forehead, my figure elongated, dwarfed by this red chair,
and my rather large hands stared at by a rare suitor. Yes, there is a kind of
optimism here, as remarked upon in a recent note from a student thanking
me for my encouragement of her fifteen years ago. One never knows
one's legacy. Perhaps there is even serenity? Enough of this. I never was
much one for looking at myself, let alone representations of that self.

I suppose my favorite part of the painting
is these washes of green, undulating and gentle.
So unlike the artist's portrayal of trees
of which there is such chatter in the cafés and elsewhere.
Is that a light in the top right of the canvas?
He seems pleased.
Perhaps we shall leave it here.
Time to go. *Goodbye, Sir. Yes, yes, the pleasure was mine.*
I will stop by the bakery and try Marie's new éclairs.
Papers to grade.
A good night beckons.

Love in the Reign of Raining Rockets

As the rockets rained on the land,
as the bombs crashed into buildings, kiosks, roads,
onto all that was animate and equally onto all that was not,
as the sirens commenced their song of terror,
as the world largely sided with the other side,
as the neighbors scurried like cockroaches into darkness,
(but never like sheep to the slaughter,
as someone observed wryly in the descent),
as the population shifted into horizontality when possible,
or hovered when not, as the parents considered the care
of their children when they themselves were underground or stranded,

someone suddenly suggested Madame Shoshanah. True, no one knew
from whence she had come or from what she had fled or how she had
become someone who whispered to souls invisible to others.
And she was getting on in years. But her person was still presentable,
with traces of refinement evident in her dress and chignon.
As was her apartment, with quick access to the ground below.
And when she was asked, she clapped her hands in delight.
She was surprised to be remembered, to be invited to contribute,
in however small a way, towards mitigating the national crisis.
She became giddy in response, to the consternation of the delegate
who was extending this offer (request) with some reluctance.

And thus the parents brought their children to Madame, if not with ease of
mind, then at least with a sense of having done the best that was possible.
But it turns out that she was outstanding with children, especially the
younger ones who still knew not to look askance upon her ways. She sang
to them songs from long ago, when there was a unity of purpose in the
country, and also songs in another language from a country far away,
passed on by her mother who eluded somehow the rockets of her day and
was herself in conversations with partners not visible to young Madame.
She played games with the children from a time before toys were automated
and danced with them in circle formations at once attainable and intricate.
Passersby marveled at the figure of Madame sheperding her flock through
detritus and din and dust to and fro shelter.

And Madame seemed to have found a new calling.
In the deluge of rockets, in the company of the children of today,
with their urgency—Sarah needs pee-pee, Uri lost his teddy bear,
Dafnah can't eat nuts—she was able to initiate new conversations.
No longer was she speaking unrecognized to her mother in her final days,
no longer was she speaking to a husband
who abandoned her before her son was born,
foraging for the causes of that abandonment,
trying to make herself more comely, more appealing,
more adaptable to an ever-growing list of demands.
Trying, trying, oh how Madame did try.

Even with her son himself, killed in a raid of some sort—
she couldn't take in the details—she found she could suddenly converse.
After years of silence, she heard the sound of his voice
as they sang together the songs of her mother.
She remembered his touch, the weight of the toddler him in her arms,
fatigued after a day of sand and sun and sea. Madame Shoshanah
remembered how handsome, how sleepy he was on the morning he left
for what was supposed to be a routine mission. The invisible friends, to
whom she had of necessity turned, who never condemned the longevity
of her grief, who never told her the period of mourning was over,
smiled, waiting in the shadows of her apartment and her mind.

1:00 A.M. Beneath Bronze Arches

And even though she was renowned throughout the region
for her soufflés supreme so sweet so savory so fluffy
some of which she filled with jams crafted from fruit—
apples, peaches, strawberries, and others—
she herself picked from orchards and patches nearby
bending and reaching in the sun for hours on end to select
only the fruit at the height of perfection
and others with cheeses whose churning
she no longer had the strength to perform
but which she oversaw with a highly attentive eye

and even though her quiches were fortified with a crust
at once flaky and sturdy
which puzzled and delighted all
for she never revealed her secrets and no sous chef was ever
present for the construction of the crust
and were filled perhaps even crammed with vegetables
she herself planted and guarded
(from the animals that creep and hop around and are resourceful
despite the fences and wire mesh and even barbed wire that she erected)
and sautéed and baked with butter and garlic and spices of all kinds

and even though everyone did think her surely a bit mad
but her food was delicious even in this region known
for the culinary arts and discerning palates
so that all of those famished for her art had to reserve a place
months in advance and even then had to wait in long lines outside
since diners were slow to savor and did not readily
surrender their hard-won seats at her tables
and there were never any left-overs to feed the homeless
so she always devoted a day a week to serve them
in the shelter over whose kitchen she was every bit as zealous

and even though many did commend her on both her high standards
and her dedication to the less fortunate
and she was awarded many honors from the industry of her peers

and from the town in which she lived and
yes I believe also the region so famed
and the photos show her just a bit dazed averted slightly from the camera
even though she always appeared at each ceremony
and thanked profusely her admirers
of whom you know now there were legion
and even though she donated most of her earnings to the shelters

and even though talents prodigious were hers
she spent her nights in a fast food restaurant in a part of town
where shootings were not uncommon and where such establishments
were often the only food sources available—the food deserts—
and there she would nurse her diet soda and her chicken tenders
and the staff would always remember her order
and she would glance at the women and all too often girls
of the street or interstate as it were
in various states of sobriety and duress
and the others stationary at tables but still wandering through night

and she would gaze outside the windows
at the cars racing past and glimpse beer cans gleaming in the weeds
and flyers fluttering past of lost children and men and women
of which she numbered herself
and the charm of a diner in a small town or a city was absent
no loneliness-rendered-into-more was here present
given the fluorescence and banality of the setting
and all that she remembered of her dreams colossal
which in the fever of her activity and awards engulfed and lashed her
retreated here and was replaced by grace and she could find restoration
before rising

The Introvert Who (Almost) Ran for Town Council

I can make a difference in this town,
she told friends. They were encouraging from the start,
pleased by her omission of the words
"I believe,"
her phrasing of desire (and ambition) as fact.
Yes, this was to be her time, of that they were sure.
They remembered the many ways,
large and small,
she had helped them,
the good she had ushered into the world.

How she had located a shelter and then a new home
for Marie,
who for years had been unable to relinquish the fists
and honey tongue of Caleb.
How she had decorated Stefan's studio apartment on thrift shop
scavenging. As if from a magazine!
How she had made sure that Markus received his disability payments
and later that he had received his meals and care … until the end.
They remembered her organizational skills and collegiality
and nodded and smiled at her over cappuccino and croissants.

She had lived her entire life here, except for a brief stint in law school
at the state university. She knew nearly everyone; everyone knew her.
She greeted folks by first name or last with a title;
she always knew which.
She could be at the diners when they were the most crowded.
She wouldn't need to research the favorite local fare;
she knew what it was and enjoyed it herself.
She could inquire after the health of parents,
spouses, and children without the prompting of an eager, underpaid
assistant or intern. This was her world, and here she was content.

She readied her platform with customary gusto and restraint.
It was to be based on fiscal prudence and civic concern.
Not the most original of approaches,

she admitted to these same friends at their next brunch,
but I will breathe new life into platitudes.
I know we can keep the central library open,
even extend Saturday hours, without raising taxes.
There will not be bile heaped upon the teachers' unions,
and yet there will be teacher accountability. There has to be.
At this, her friends murmured approval.

And one day walking home from work in what passed for a skyscraper in
this town although the heavens towered far above and were not scraped at
all today but were streaked with violet and silver and the wind blew used
car sales flyers across the plaza and she hurried to escape the drear into
her slim-fronted townhouse, she knew she couldn't do it. She couldn't
transition from brunch table to back room. She didn't have the right
connections forged at the right schools. She didn't have a Rolodex
with the right names. She didn't have a light touch with donors;
she hated to grovel. Most of all, she hated to press the flesh,
work the room, kiss babies, smile into cameras.

Who had she been kidding with this pie-in-the-sky dream?
She placed her keys in the bowl on the vestibule table, pleased by the lack
of mirror above so she wouldn't have to see her graying hair which
she refused to dye and by the lack of prying eyes which sent her into
jitters and would follow her if she refused to let go of the pie which her
mother had warned her against and which now called out to her from the
refrigerator. Cinnamon apple, to be precise, purchased from the bakery
downtown. And although her figure was still trim, tonight, with its
demons of celestial pie relinquished, would not be a night of moderation
of earthly pie. There might even be vanilla ice cream involved.

And she knew that there were still other matters the prying eyes
would uncover that were best left unexposed, ones that an accomplished
middle-aged woman couldn't bear to face and which would not survive
ruthless scrutiny. And though she was weary of being the woman in the
background of the photograph who could always be depended upon
for the correct fact sheet, who had read up on every issue at hand,
who would remain obscure to the headline readers if not to the wonks
aware of the machinations behind the scenes, she was grateful still
for the affection of friends, who would surely understand her decision,
and for the years, out of the limelight and in the quiet, remaining to her.

Cautionary Tale

She was once so lovely,
with auburn waves cascading down her tapered back,
skin as if skimmed by pearls.
Well, maybe not lovely exactly, but attractive. Striking.
Remember how men gaped as she walked down the street.
Yes, even in Borough Park; yes, even in Monsey.
Only now look at her: the curves squared, the waves in retreat.
Oy nebekh, nebekh. Such a *nebekh.*

She was once so elegant,
always in the right ensemble, with the right accessories.
Well, maybe not elegant exactly, but different. Unusual.
Remember the polka dotted dress she wore to my Shloymi's bar mitzvah
and those pink beads. Even at Etti *zikhroyne livrokhe*'s funeral,
her lilac suit was so comforting, so soft when I hugged her afterwards.
Only now look at her, schlepping to market in housecoat and slippers.
Oy nebekh, nebekh. Such a *nebekh.*

She was once so saintly,
always with the right word, a way of creating ease.
Well, maybe not saintly exactly, but kind. Good.
Remember how she used to take the kids from school when I had to work.
When Meyer was in the hospital, she brought hot meals for all of us.
With dessert too!
Only now she makes everyone nervous; did you see how they look away?
Oy nebekh, nebekh. Such a *nebekh.*

She was once so brilliant,
always with the right answer, the solution to the problem.
Well, maybe not brilliant exactly, but smart. Disciplined.
She knew whole *parshes* by heart yet never boasted.
Remember how the teachers of the secular subjects in *Beys Yankev*
secretly begged her to apply to college. But she couldn't. She wouldn't.
Only now she can barely hold on to her city job.
Oy nebekh, nebekh. Such a *nebekh.*

She was once the Wonder Girl of 13th Avenue,
telling parables of our Righteous Ones,
hurrying to greet the Sabbath Queen after shopping for her parents and
making the *tsholnt* and mopping the floors. But now she is alone
in a rented room subsidized by the *gmiles-khesed*.
But we shouldn't question; this is how it goes sometimes.
I want you to know that I *davened* for her at the *Meores hamakhpeyle*.
Oy nebekh, nebekh. Such a *nebekh.*

So turn left and here we are; that's our house.
Yes, right next to the bakery. You've never had such *mandlbroyt*!
Am I lucky or what!
Still, it was good to see her, wasn't it?
Thank you so much. *Nor af simkhes. Al dos guts.*
Listen, maybe invite her for a Shabbas meal,
maybe you know of someone for her.
You just never know. Stranger things have happened.

––––––––––

oy nebekh (Yiddish): oh, what a pity!, poor thing!
zikhroyne livrokhe (Yiddish, of Hebrew origin): of blessed memory
parshes (Yiddish, of Hebrew origin: weekly Torah portions
Beys Yankev (Yiddish, of Hebrew origin): literally the house of Jacob,
the name of an Orthodox school system for girls
tsholnt (Yiddish): stew, eaten on the Sabbath
gmiles-khesed (Yiddish, of Hebrew origin): charitable association
daven (Yiddish): pray
Meores hamakhpeyle (Yiddish, of Hebrew origin): the tomb of the
Matriarchs and the Patriarchs located in Hebron
mandlbroyt (Yiddish): almond bread, similar to biscotti
nor af simkhes (Yiddish): only on joyful occasions
al dos guts (Yiddish): all the best

זי איז אַ מאָל געווען דאָס ווונדער-מיידל פון דער 13טער עוועניו,
דערצײלנדיק משלים פון אונדזערע צדיקים,
זיך געאײַלט צו באַגריסן די שבת-מלכה נאָכן גײן אין מאַרק פאַר טאַטע-מאַמע און
קאָכן טשאָלנט און וואַשן די פּאָדלאָגע. אָבער איצט איז זי אַלײן
אין אַ געדונגענעם צימער באַצאָלט פון דעם גמילות-חסד.
אָבער פרעגן טאָר מען ניט; אַזוי גײט עס אַ מאָל.
זײ וויסן אַז כ'האָב געדאַוונט פאַר איר בײַ דער מערת-המכפלה.
אוי נעבעך, נעבעך. אַזאַ נעבעך.

איז דרײַ זיך דאָ אַרײַן לינקס און מיר זײַנען שוין דאָ; אָט איז אונדזער הויז.
יאָ, פּונקט לעבן דער בעקערײַ. אַזאַ מאָנדלברויט האָסטו נאָך קײן מאָל
ניט פאַרזוכט!
ניט אומזיסט זאָגט מען אַז איך האָב מזל!
אָבער ס'איז געווען גוט זי צו זען, איאָ?
אַ האַרציקן דאַנק. נאָר אויף שׂימחות. כּל-טובֿ.
הער זיך אײַן, אפֿשר קענסטו זי פאַרבעטן אויף אַ שבת-סעודה,
אפֿשר קענסטו עמעצער פאַר איר.
מע קען קײן מאָל ניט וויסן. דאַכט זיך מער אויסטערלישע זאַכן זײַנען זיכער געשעהן.

משל-אַזהרה

זי איז אַ מאָל געווען אַזוי שײן,
מיט רויט-ברוינע האָר אַראָפּכוואַליענדיק אויף איר שלאַנקן רוקן,
די הויט אַזוי ווי געלײשט מיט פּערל.
נו, אפֿשר ניט שײן גענוי, אָבער צוציענדיק. מערקווערדיק.
געדענקסט ווי מענער האָבן געגאַפֿט בשעת זי האָט שפּאַצירט אין גאַס.
יאָ, אַפֿילו אין באָראַ-פּאַרק, יאָ, אַפֿילו אין מאָנסי.
נאָר גיב איצט אַ קוק אויף איר: די בײגן פֿון איר גוף זײנען שאַרפֿער געוואָרן,
די האָר כוואַליען זיך צוריק.
אוי נעבעך, נעבעך. אַזאַ נעבעך.

זי איז אַ מאָל געווען אַזוי עלעגאַנט,
אַלע מאָל פֿאַסיק-געקלײדט, אַלע פּיטשעווקעס ווי געהעריק.
נו, אפֿשר ניט עלעגאַנט גענוי, אָבער אַנדערש. ניט געוויינטלעך.
געדענקסט דאָס באַפֿינטלטע קלײד וואָס זי האָט געטראָגן אויף שלומיס בר-מיצווה,
און יענע רעזעווע קרעלן. אַפֿילו אויף עטי זכרונה לברכהס לוויה
איז איר אָנצוג געווען אַזאַ טרייסט, אַזוי ווייך ווען איך האָב זי שפּעטער אַרוקגענומען.
נאָר גיב איצט אַ קוק אויף איר, זיך שלעפֿנדיק אין מאַרק אין שלאָפֿראָק און שטעקשיך.
אוי נעבעך, נעבעך. אַזאַ נעבעך.

זי איז אַ מאָל געווען אַזוי הײליק,
אַלע מאָל אַ פֿאַסיק ווערט, אַן אופֿן שאַפֿן באַקוועמקייט.
נו, אפֿשר ניט הײליק גענוי, אָבער האַרציק. גוט.
געדענקסט ווי זי האָט אַהיימגענומען די קינדער פֿון חדר ווען כ׳האָב געדאַרפֿט אַרבעטן.
ווען מאיר איז געגעבן אין שפּיטאָל איז האָט זי אונדז אַלע געבראַכט הייסע מאָלצייטן.
מיט דעסערט אויך!
נאָר איצט דענערווירט זי יעדערן; האָסטו געזען ווי מע קוקט אַוועק?
אוי נעבעך, נעבעך. אַזאַ נעבעך.

זי איז אַ מאָל געווען אַזאַ עילוי,
אַלע מאָל מיט דער ריכטיקער תשובה, דעם באַשייד אויף דער פּראָבלעם.
נו, אפֿשר ניט פּונקט אַן עילוי, אָבער קלוג. דיסציפּלינירט.
זי האָט געקענט גאַנצע פּרשיות פֿון אויסנווייניק אָבער האָט זיך מאָל ניט באַרימט.
געדענקסט ווי אַזוי די לעררינס פֿון די וועלטלעכע-לימודים אין בית-יעקבֿ האָבן
זי סודותדיק זיך געבעטן
אין שיקן אַן אַפּליקאַציע אויף אוניווערסיטעט. אָבער זי האָט ניט געקענט. זי
וואָלט דאָס ניט געטאָן.
נאָר איצט קוים וואָס זי קען האַלטן איר שטעלע מיט דער שטאָט-רעגירונג.
אוי נעבעך, נעבעך. אַזאַ נעבעך.

In Blue Moonlight

It isn't because I give such good head, you know, I tell my sister,
both of us surrounded by her pastries. I admire her flair with the oven,
her mastery of the science of it all—from the simple moistness of her
brownies to the intricacy of her layer cake, embraced by gossamer
frosting. She, with her first-class degree in physics, is at last making
good use of her education. Her eyebrows furrow in disgust,
not at my erotic bluster, but at my "self-abasement,"
my contentment with crumbs. She needn't state it,
just as Father never needed to state his displeasure
with her career choice. It is and was all too apparent.

Of course, there is no response. She sets down her cream puff and gazes
above me, through the window, to the air shaft and the brick wall of the
tenement opposite. She is reminded suddenly of an appointment, how
she has to fetch Mirah from play group, then send her webmaster some
cake photos. In short, she is reminded of why she must stay away from
me, of why her visits to me are so rare and mine to her rarer still.
I escort her to the door and shiver in relief at its closing,
at the click of her stilettos down the stairs.
Jimmy Choos? I forgot to ask; I do care about such things,
however beyond my means they are.

I look around at the pastry panorama; I will donate it to the busybody
neighbor. Perhaps she will be less likely to tsk-tsk at him
through a crack in the door as he goes downstairs,
or through lace curtains as he drives away. Perhaps. I won't count on it.
In any case, I can't eat any of this. I need to maintain my figure.
Suddenly, with my sister gone, my confidence has ebbed.
Truth be told, I can't always be sure of his arrival,
when his wife might be away,
when his flight delays or his jetlag will have their way,
when, from among his many calls to return, he might choose mine.

No, I don't wait for him exactly. I have my work—conveying the glory
of the Torah and Hebrew grammar to the youth of the international set,
an occasional star twinkling among them and my writing, hunched over
the *Rabbinic Bible* and commentaries long into morning. All that's

missing is a cat in the window to complete the scene. Alas there once was
one, but I had to give Blue away. How I miss dear Blue! But he is
allergic, you see. And so I had to choose. In the classroom or at
conferences, at the tavern with the regulars, but especially after mastering
the nuances of a particularly thorny passage, I am destitute with desire
for him. Destitute as in without home, adrift.

Would that it were not so. Would that there were another whose hands,
(massive, gentle), could so electrify me; whose anecdotes, (pointedly
harvested from the antics of NGOs), could so make me smile, of whose
words of need whispered in my skin I would never tire. But there is not.
I have been with him these many years. I know that if this does continue,
this is how it will continue. I know too every step of his wife's descent,
every nuance of their despair at her barrenness,
I know his tears at midnight over each failed visit to yet another charlatan.
This all I know.
And still he comes to me. And still I welcome him.

On a Given Sunday

The senator from a state renowned for its cancer-causing products
has just finished the Sabbath dinner. After loosening his belt a
notch or two (Delia truly has perfected her brisket and cornbread), he
decides to take time to reflect on today's sermon in the privacy of his
study. Perhaps too to reflect on the arrival into the congregation
of a mysterious young man, whose lines and curves were,
beneath summer linen and seersucker, utterly bewitching.
And he is reluctant, these hours later, to break that spell.

Gathering himself, the senator will have to monitor the day's progress—
the bills, the constituents' missives, the (dreaded) donor calls from those
who want what they claim only he can give … at least for now.
That is, if he does exactly as they "suggest", which today,
given the brisket and the cornbread, he is largely wont to do.
He knows that this is the Day of Rest, but the public must be served.
And Mae is visiting the ladies to plan a fund raising benefit for …
He wishes he could remember the inspiration for Mae's current initiative.

And of course Delia is still here, cleaning in the kitchen. Humming
hymns under breath no doubt. Dear, devoted Delia. With them all these
years. With good reason to skedaddle, he acknowledges. Mae has never
been easy, and the years have only hardened her ways. He wonders how
Delia makes ends meet; all too aware is he of the limits of his largesse.
Expectations managed, he supposes, something with which he, despite
his power, is all too familiar. Wealth shall not follow us into earth,
the preacher had said earlier, declining to note its value in the today.

Delia knows not to interrupt him in his study, his sanctuary.
Only he can clean it, he insists. If his listless fanning of the duster can be
called "cleaning." And you won't find what you'd think you'd find.
There are no images locked away in drawers, no clean supply of
hand towels. Mostly he prefers reverie. He thinks of the preacher's
invective against abomination, or he should say "invectives" for he
has heard them since he was a little boy, comprehending, knowing,
trembling in sky blue shorts that clung to the pew benches.

How he has despised that little boy, all too grateful for the energy supplied
by his neighbors who became his constituents, how he eagerly joined them
repeatedly, rapturously even, in the failed erasure of that little boy. Sometimes he wonders how *he* hasn't skedaddled. A word he finds ridiculous
but nevertheless alluring. He might have, too, in this day and age. Times
are changing. Or are they? Some would feign surprise; others would claim
they'd seen the signs all along. Sometimes he thinks, if I had just returned
the gaze of X, or followed Y down the alley behind the haberdashery ...

Still, what would (have) become of Mae? Mae, whose grief at the silence
coursing from the nursery, has left her submerged in good works. And
what would become of the images he has so carefully cultivated—the
men who circulate through gray, who open doors only to close them—
as he strokes the hand of Mae, charitable plans in hand, in the newly
renovated parlor, as he accompanies Mae to her ever lightless room, as
the wave of Delia's sacred song (and the clatter of heirloom cutlery)
carries him, breathless, to the cluttered visions of his own sanctuary.

Revolutionaries on Holiday

Oskar had suggested that they locate a village near the border,
one nestled into the mountains, with stairs winding every which way
and streets with obscure names sprinkled with cafés from which
pumpernickel and Streuselkuchen could be procured and savored.
He had had several such villages recommended to him by a comrade
at a rally last month and had decided on just the one for their stay.
But he had insisted instead on this cabin by the lake,
where the air would be crisp
and the moon would pierce the water's lacquered facade
and the creatures of the forest would be the only witnesses to their love,
which he liked to think of not as forbidden,
but as little understood.

And now unpacking their valises in the pink of dusk,
Oskar outside chopping wood, he was not sorry he had done so,
was even pleased he had insisted on this destination.
It was unusual for him to counter Oskar's suggestions, which, of course,
weren't really suggestions at all. True, there might be repercussions back
home in their garret lodgings in the city adjacent to several streetcar
lines, with bells pealing into night. A verbal lashing,
or perhaps a physical one. But here tonight, they could set
aside the broadsides and manifestoes and pamphlets and speeches yet to
be written, the workers yet to be organized, the hope yet to be
uncovered and foregrounded amidst the peril of acquiescence.
The lake, the birches would see to that.

And yet even here he could not help but think of those repercussions.
Oskar would tersely suggest that the cabin,
with its seclusion and views,
had been too extravagant, especially now with the Financial Crisis
and so many out of work and evicted from their homes
and funds needed for shelters and soup kitchens
and to slake the thirst of their new printing press.
Oskar would become yet more rigid with the household expenses.
And other comrades might cast sidelong glances after a meeting
as he (rather than Oskar) praised the clarity of the lake's waters,

and recounted how they had both felt so restored in its embrace.
And he would guide the conversation to waters of greater stillness.

And here was Oskar now entering the cabin from the pines beyond,
his body perspiring, his biceps knotty and intricate around the kindling,
the hallelujah of him,
moving about in a halo of health and resolve,
starting a fire now building momentum,
sampling the stew now beginning to simmer on the stove.
And here were Oskar's arms around him, pulling closer,
and beyond were the eyes of a doe gleaming in crepuscule,
and he delighted in the day's braiding of the ordinary and the extraordinary,
and he shivered with delight in the tracing of Oskar's hands over his back
and in anticipation of the welts likely to flower.

Alley Apparition (without Pierogis)

When I glimpsed strangers making out in the alley behind the diner
my body leaden with kashe varnishkes my veins stained by borscht
the cobblestones glittering in October mist
his hands flitting over her thighs her breasts pausing flitting again
as if they could find no rest then finally darting up to her hair
semi-kempt and her head upturned to stars twinkling in indifference

I thought achingly of Muffy and the hunger to be (the) other
to shed WASP-ness
to feed upper crusts to the swans decorous yet militant
on the mirrored lake not in Central Park
but somewhere in Westport or Greenwich …
or whichever genteel hamlet from which Muffy emanated

and I thought too of Mama and her pierogis renowned throughout the
neighborhood so fluffy were they as if they had never
been dipped in oil at all but in light itself golden
and of the quarrels terrible in their quiet and march towards oblivion
we—Papa and I—engaged in after dinner
on the likelihood ever so slim of my earning an artistic living wage

and of the smokestacks curdling outside our rented rowhouse
the stench of the steel foundries clotting our lungs
and the soot coating everything except the stoop that Mama polished daily
and her pierogis which somehow eluded it all ensuring that I would never
consume pierogis again and I haven't these many years
even tonight and never even with Muffy

whom I met soon after my arrival in the big city the shiny apple
at a party dense with ambition and the theories of the day—
"poststructuralist" swooping through the boozy chatter—where neither of
us knew a soul and so we marveled at how we were here and meant to be
together even if Muffy was then a lesbian feminist separatist
and I—what was I? a nancy boy no a nancy waif from the industrial west
who was just so relieved to be away from the smokestacks
and my father's disappointment vast and uncontained

that I wept with joy into her already too thin neck
confident that our disheveled joy would carry the day for
sure was she that the members of her collective would be amused by me
a bright golden plaything only they were not most definitely not

and Muffy was thus evicted by the hardening of ideology landing on my
doorstep and we said what fun and it was so for a while with late breakfast
of coffee and cigarettes and she tried to find her way into our parties the
wit ironic self-deprecating and the ogling of baseball players but was
not amused and turned away returning later less present more vacant
and I began to worry only Muffy assured me not to and from there

it happened so quickly she less and less and I nudging and frantic
and some pretty rough trade arriving suddenly in the loft
and however sexy sometimes they I began to fear for her and for me
and then there was a trailing off of her and so we went searching for her
calling out Muffy! Muffy! not into forest primeval but along the piers
and in dens of this and that iniquity where we had last gotten word

imbuing with love her name (that wasn't a nickname) that she so despised
but would not change sculpting those syllables outward into something
altogether dear only Muffy was not to be the trails led nowhere despite the
arrival of her parents bejeweled coiffed even in terror-on-the-verge-of-
grief and the police impassive none too pleased with us surveying the
male nudes and the manifestoes and petitions for this or that in Muffy's

papers the unsavory sorts that only the epicenter can offer all converging
on nada and yet I never gave up on the parties even now when the closet
and its brand of humor are so unfashionable and even now when I can't
bring myself to order pierogis I cannot forget Muffy her laugh laced with
blue her insistence that talk is not cheap her dream of a world
without brutality how once she kissed me on the lips below the El train

tracks before dawn so that when I landed here in this alley behind this
diner alongside the skittering of rats was that a raccoon and spying on this
couple my heart skipping a beat at the shape of her slouch the movement
of moon only it wasn't of course it wasn't there were only glares of
fury and borscht and kashe varnishkes rising spewing into the dumpster
and still no Muffy but only these stars twinkling against her absence

In Bed with the Widow Empress

Dwarfed by fur and outsized baubles, she sits at the center of a Lucite
round table and delivers witticisms on the sartorial mishaps of the starlets,
sending her minions into peals of joyless cackling.
Her face has been stretched and tucked and tweezed over the years,
underlining the unsmiling delivery of her barbs and providing fodder for
her self-deprecating humor which reverberates with ferocity through the
evening. Her make-up, applied with a scholarly precision, exacerbates
her chief geisha appearance. She would have it no other way.

Under the lash of her tongue, the unsuccessful starlets emerge as victims
of folly, or at the very list, tarnished. For all the advisors, for all the
eagerness of the designers to use their bodies as billboards, the starlets
have failed. They might have failed with a hue that is garish; they might
have failed with a hue that clashes with skin tone; they might have
failed with a style that insults body shape utterly. There might have been
errors in accessories or chignon or even shoes. It really is impossible to
enumerate the many ways in which the starlets might have failed.

Their poise on the scarlet carpet, however practiced, will be dismissed.
Even the pleasure of gaining access to the most elite post-
extravaganza bacchanalia will ring hollow. Tomorrow the tabloids will
brandish the photos. As her edicts are broadcast, the starlets will retreat,
shivering in shame. Or they will (regretfully) fire a hapless assistant. Or
they will feign indifference, braving the civility in the boutiques
and the blather in the bars. There are always options, but
whatever their path, they will not escape unscathed from the royal lashing.

The widow empress will disrobe alone later in an apartment as baroque
as her costume tonight. She, of course, has not been invited to the
extravaganza or to any of the aforementioned intoxications.
She removes from her newly unwithered neck her necklace, splurged
on after a spree of sold-out dinner theater gigs in the provinces.
As the rubies clatter onto her dressing table, she remembers her mother's
hopes for her whispered at bedtime — that she might find a
husband and build a large family under a suburban canopy of trees,

that she might find security and nurture understatement in all things.
She remembers knowing precisely when her mother was reaching
for a brandy snifter below as she awaited a husband who would
stagger in near dawn or beyond. She remembers the splash of the
brandy on the rocks in her mother's trembling hand. She remembers
and she smiles for neither security nor understatement has she found.
No one since her mother has ever told her she is gorgeous;
no one has ever said, *without you I cannot live.*

And she has no illusions that anyone ever will.
Despite the tautness of her skin, she clearly wasn't born yesterday.
The rubies and other jewels may vanish as suddenly as her husband;
the minions will likely tire of her once she fails to amuse them.
Still she remembers, still she smiles.
Still she spins, still she reaches, still she rifles through the
drawers of bon-mots, one-liners, jokes, and puns,
all cataloged with care, she ever a dervish for inspiration.

Still the widow empress wills
the skewer into sharpness
and the eternal adoration of the fans
(at least until she can retire if ever she can),
and somewhere, somewhere,
anywhere, anywhere,
a glimpse of her parents,
entwined in embrace, content together in old age.

Return of the Repressed

Leaves, long since no-longer-gold, flutter across the circular drive.
You observe that its shape so suitable for a horse-drawn carriage or a
Model T seems less so for a lone straggler without a suitcase or valise.
Your heels, although flat and without taps, sound thunderous to your ear
on edge. The wind whisks echoes of your steps into its own bitter refrain.
Perhaps you shouldn't be here, you would once have thought.

The shrubbery and foliage, formerly the pride of the neighborhood, shiver
raggedly across a pouting sky. Weeds and unidentified scrub growth
flourish madly. You think, I can't bear to look up to see the state of the
shutters and the cupola from where Sylvie declaimed your new oratory
to unseen adoring crowds. This was where Sylvie mastered inflection;
this was where you came to accept backdrop, or to drop back.

But you do look up as if drawn by a force beyond yourself. And your
worst fears are confirmed. There's no way around it—the shutters are
chipped, lopsided, missing many louvers, hanging by a rusty thread as it
were. The cupola, missing its signature pointed roof and many railings,
has met an even worse fate. You are not surprised, even if you wish you
had maintained a level gaze. You've always fetishized neutrality.

You approach the front door, its carvings strangely still gleaming. You
look into its high window. Despite the gray of the day, sunlight is
refracted through stained glass windows above the circular staircase.
You strain for echoes of Thanksgiving dinners past in the room just to
the staircase's left. You make out the click of silver against china,
the communication through gesture, the interplay of staccato and silence.

You reach for the cranberry sauce that your mother flecked so sparingly
with cinnamon and cloves. Your mouth waters, despite your father's
invocations against excess. This time you will not be lauded for your
discipline. You hear the chimes of Sylvie's laughter at this display of
bravura; you glimpse the flash of her auburn locks as she floats up the
stairs. Even here, even now in this rust sun, Sylvie will become the day.

The Problem of Cacophony

Malvinia remembers song.
She remembers the light of her mother's hand on her shoulder
steering her through tall grass, to the siren call of the organ,
to praise surging from a threadbare white building
to which she and her mother were forbidden entry.
She remembered how they both crouched in the weeds to be near,
her mother's breath damp and scalding in her ear as she sang in acclaim
of His beneficence and the certainty of their place among the rewarded.

Malvinia remembers song.
She remembers the ditties of men as they lurched up the stairs and rapped
on the door of their shack. She remembers the shapes of those treads, the
shatter of those raps, the cadences of those ditties before those raps,
the murmuring, the negotiation, her mother telling her to "hide" behind
the curtain, then the bedsprings squeaking, then the words or the hush
that followed. Whether there would in fact be words or hush.
Malvinia always knew. Malvinia always remembered.

Malvinia remembers song.
She remembers songs from her first phonograph,
when she swore her path would be different, her own entirely.
She remembers songs of customers arriving late,
the refrains as she wiped the countertops of mustard, as she scoured the
cups of coffee dust. She remembers melodic lines as she lay unmoving
on the floor of her room gradually reddening as the door closed finally
behind he who might have been if he could only have been otherwise.

Malvinia remembers song.
She remembers all of these songs or parts of them—excerpts, snippets,
strands. Call them what you will. They converge in a crescendo of
confusion; they create thunder in her cosmos.
She bows her head; she shouts! These are what devour Malvinia.
These are what have sustained Malvinia. These are what sustain her still
as she sings to pedestrians passing, as she smiles at the few who drop
coins into her paper cup, the fewer still who look up in so doing.

Refugees from Little League

When gazing absently out the kitchen window while washing dishes
or when grunting on her knees scrubbing linoleum floors or when driving
her son to little league practice or when watching the games
which nearly always drove her to smoke so tedious were they to her
and yet she always did embrace him through his brink-of-tears even as
she wondered why he insisted on this ordeal three times a week
year after year when all he really wanted was to wear dresses and play
with the neighbor girl's dolls, she never thought they'd end up here.

Rather, she always thought she'd bring them to a garret in the city. Like
the heroines in her favorite novels, she would drift through a string of
affairs ever less loving. She would work at night, after she'd tuck him
into bed, in those palatial office buildings scrubbing the marble floors
nearly invisible to the executives and their underlings. And she would find
sustenance in the lentil soup on the table, in the acceptance of her son in
the throng, in the hairy bodies that would occasionally come to envelop her,
in the shadow play on the sloped ceiling on nights when they did not.

But one day instead of little league she drove them past the diamond
and far further yet. At dusk they found themselves in a wood.
She couldn't believe they were only a day away from the strip malls
and the fast food chains and the stares. And this was here: a vast expanse
of trees soaring out of loamy earth. She was suddenly as if a dog en route
to a jackpot of truffles. She fell to the ground to kiss and inhale its
blackness. Her son followed suit, and as suddenly, as if a puppy.
Only then did she consider them as exiles ingathering, gathering in.

And so they are at last here. It's not as if they've never left,
but as if they are only now discovering their truly essential location.
They marvel at the foliage everywhere.
Ferns? Ivy? Weeds? She was sure there was lavender nearby.
She wished she had been a more diligent botany student.
She wished she had been a better girl scout. Her son, of course,
would be of no use in that way. Still, she would come to know them.
They both would, of that she was certain. In due time.

She would learn to forage—which berries to gather, which to avoid.
She would learn to protect her young. She would adapt; again they both
would. And if the forest began to shrink, she would move, like the bears,
deer, and raccoons before and alongside her, back into the suburbs,
to forage with her newly honed olfactory skills. But this was not the time
for that. The time now was for satisfying the hunger that had overtaken
them and for creating shelter. She saw a hollow in a gnarled oak ahead
that would surely welcome them.

Dear reader, dear listener, there is so much more to tell about our pair.
Having heard that such "back to the land" tales have rarely ended well,
you may wonder if their transformation was as complete as this poem
suggests. For example, did her hair, once kept in the most envied chignon
of the neighborhood, become scraggly? Now that she would no longer
forage in estate sales and thrift shops, would she be able to maintain her
elegance? Perhaps she reinvented herself in branches, leaves, and flowers
artfully woven, a kind of woodland chic, if you will.

You may wonder if our son found material to create dolls
or whether he still wished to play with dolls at all.
You may wonder if our mother found partners for her own amusement,
as was once her wont. You may wonder if she found lavender
and berries and sustenance for herself and her child.
Perhaps she stumbled upon the candy trails left in earlier fairy tales?
And you will surely wonder about the causes of the flight
that resulted in this most improbable of transformations.

These, dear reader, dear listener, are all good questions,
and I would certainly not wish to discourage curiosity and probing.
But alas their answers extend beyond the parameters of this poem.
Perhaps you hear will hear rustling in the vale beyond on your next hike.
Or perhaps you will simply sense their presence, unsettled, quicksilver
through the birches. And you must content yourself with that. Just that.
Do not try to speak to them; do not disturb their equilibrium so hard won.
Let them be. Dear reader, dear listener, let them go.

צייט אויף דעם. איצט מוז זי געבן צו עסן דעם הונגער וואָס האָט זיי איבערגענומען
און שאַפֿן אַ מיקלט. זי האָט געזען אַ חלל אין אַ סוקאַטען דעמב אין פֿאָראויס
וואָס וואָלט זיי זיכער באַגריסט.

טײַערער לייענער, טײַערער צוהערער, פֿאַראַן נאָך אַ סך צו זאָגן וועגן אונדזער פּאַרל.
אַזוי ווי איר האָט מסתּמא געהערט אז אַזעלכע "צוריק צום ערד" מעשׂיות זײַנען ניט אַלע
מאָל געקומען צו אַ גוטן סוף,
וועט איר אפֿשר פֿרעגן צי זייער גליגול איז געווען אַזוי טאַטאַל ווי דאָס ליד
לייגט פֿאָר. למשל, זײַנען איר האָר, אַמאָל געהאַלטן אין אַ שינײַאָן
וואָס דער גאַנצער געגנט האָט מקנא געווען, געוואָרן צעשׂויבערט? איצט אַז זי וועט ניט
קענען זוכן אין די אַלערליי געשעפֿטן פֿון גענוצטע חפֿצים, וועט זי קענען אָנהאַלטן איר
עלעגאַנץ? אפֿשר האָט זי זיך אויפֿס ניט אויסגעטראַכט אין צוזיבן, בלעטער,
און בלומען קינסטלעריש אויסגעוועבט, אַ מין וואַלדשיק, אַזוי צו זאָגן.

איר וועט זיך פֿרעגן צי אונדזער זון האָט געפֿונען שטאָף אויף צו באַשאַפֿן ליאַלקעס
אָדער צי ער האָט בכלל נאָך אַלץ געוואַלט שפּילן מיט ליאַלקעס.
איר וועט זיך פֿרעגן צי אונדזער מאַמע האָט געפֿונען שותּפֿים פֿאַר איר פֿאַרווײַלונג,
ווי איז אַמאָל געווען איר שטײַגער. איר וועט זיך אפֿשר פֿרעגן צי זי האָט געפֿונען לאַוונענדער
און יאַגדעס און עסן פֿאַר זיך אַליין און דאָס קינד.
אפֿשר האָט זי זיך אָנגעטראַפֿן אויף די זיסוואַרג–וועגן איבערגעלאָזט אין מעשׂהלעך פֿון אַ מאָל?
און איר וועט זיך פֿרעגן וועגן די סיבות פֿון איר אַנטלויפֿן
וואָס האָט זיך אויסגעלאָזט אין אַ טראַנספֿאָרמאַציע וואָס לייגט זיך אין גאַנצן ניט אויפֿן שׂכל.

אָט די קשיות, טײַערער לייענער, טײַערער צוהערער, זײַנען אַלע גוטע קשיות,
און איך וואָלט זיכער ניט געוואָלט אַנטמוטיקן נײַגער און בדיקה.
אָבער צום באַדיערן די ענטפֿערס געפֿינען זיך מחוץ די גרענעצן פֿון דעם ליד.
אפֿשר וועט איר אַמאָל הערן אַ שאַרקן אינעם טאָל אין דער ווטײטנס אויף אײַער
קומענדיקן שפּאַציר.
אָדער אפֿשר וועט איר זיי פּשוט פֿילן, אָמרויק, קווועקזילבער
דורך די בערעזעס. און איר וועט זיך מוזן באַפֿרײדיקן מיט דעם. נאָר מיט דעם.
פֿרוווט ניט רעדן מיט זיי; שטערט ניט זייער אַזוי שווער פֿאַרדינטער גלײַכוואָג.
לאָזט זיי צו רו. טײַערער לייענער, טײַערער צוהערער, לאָזט זיי אָפּ.

פּליטים פֿון קינדער-בייסבאָל

אַרויסקוקנדיק צעטראָגן פֿונעם קיכפֿענצטער וואַשנדיק כּלים
אָדער בורטשענדיק אויף די קניען אויסשטשערונדיק לינאָלייַ-דילן אָדער צופֿירנדיק
איר זון אויף קינדער-בייסבאָל מאַטשן אָדער קוקנדיק אויף די מאַטשן אַליין
וואָס האָבן זי געפֿירט כּמעט אַלע מאָל צו רייכערן אַזוי נונדע זיַנען זיי איר געווען
און דאָך האָט זי אים אַלע מאָל אַרומגענומען ווען זי האָט ער האָט געהאַלטן ביַ טרערן אַפֿילו ווען
זי האָט זיך געפֿרעגט פֿאַר וואָס ער האָט זיך איינגעשפּאַרט אויף דעם אָפּקומעניש דריַ מאָל אַ וואָך
יאָר נאָך יאָר ווען ער האָט באמת נאָר געוואָלט טראַגן קליידלעך און שפּילן
מיטן שכנס טאָכטערס ליאַלקעס, האָט זי זיך קיין מאָל ניט גערעכנט אַז זיי וועלן דערגיין אַהער.

גיכער האָט זי אַלע מאָל געמיינט אַז זי וועט זיי באַזעצן אין אַ בוידעמשטיבל ערגעץ אין שטאָט. אַזוי ווי
די העלדינס פֿון אירע באַליבסטע ראָמאַנען וואָלט זי זיך געטראָגן דורך אַ סעריע
ראָמאַנען מיט וואָס אַ מאָל ווייניקער ליבע. זי וואָלט געאַרבעט ביַ נאַכט, נאָך דעם וואָלט זי
אים געלייגט שלאָפֿן, אין די קעניגלעכע בנינים אויסשטשערונדיק די מאַרמערנע דילן
כּמעט אומזעעוודיק די עקזעקוטיוון און זייערע אונטערטעניקע. און זי וואָלט זיך
געשטיצט אויף דער לינדז-זוף אויפֿן טיש, אינעם אָנעם פֿון איר זון אין
דער שטאָט, אין די האָריקע גופֿים וואָס וואָלטן זעלטן געקומען זי אײנהילן,
אין דער שאָטן-שפּיל אויף דער משופּעדיקער סטעליע במשך די נעכט ווען געקומען זיַנען זיי ניט.

אָבער איין טאָג אַנשטאָט קינדער-בייסבאָל האָט זי זיי פֿאַרביַגעפֿירט דעם בייסבאָל-"דיאַמאַנט"
און נאָך אַ סך אַ וויַטער. ביַ בין-השמשות האָבן זיי זיך געפֿונען אין אַ וואַלד.
זי האָט קוים געגלייבט אַז זיי זיַנען נאָר איין טאָג אַוועק פֿון די קראַמען-צענטערס
און די גיך-עסן רעסטאָראַנען און זייערע גלאַצן. און אָט דאָס איז דאָ געווען: ביַמער רחבֿותדיק
אויסגעשפּרייט אַרויספֿשוועעבנדיק פֿון גיביקער ערד. זי איז פּלוצעם געוואָרן ווי אַ הונט אויפֿן וועג
צו אַ שפֿע פֿון זעלטענע שוואָמען. איר זון האָט זי נאָכגעטאָן, און פּונקט אַזוי פּלוצעם, אַזוי ווי אַ הינטל.
נאָר אינעם מאָמענט האָט זי זיי באַטראַכט ווי פֿאַרשיקטע אַריַנקומענדיק, קומענדיק אַריַן.

איז זיַנען זיי שוין סוף-כּל-סוף דאָ. ס'איז ניט אַזוי ווי זיי זיַנען קיין מאָל ניט אַוועק,
נאָר אַזוי ווי זיי אַנטדעקן ערשט איצט זייער עיקרדיקן אָרט.
זיי באַוווּנדערן דאָס געבלעטער וואָס געפֿינט זיך אומעטום.
פֿעדערגראָאַזן? ווילדער וויַן? ווילדגראַזן? זי איז געוווּן זיכער אַז לאָוונדער איז נאָענט.
הלוואַי וואָלט זי געהאַט געווען אַ פֿליַסיקערע באָטאַניק-סטודענדקע.
הלוואַי וואָלט זי געהאַט געווען אַ בעסערע סקויטע. איר זון וואָלט, פֿאַרשטייט
זיך, ניט געקענט העלפֿן מיט דעם. דאָך וואָלט זי מיט דער צײַט זיך באַקענט מיט זיי.
זיי ביידע וואָלט זיך מיט זיי באַקענט, וועגן דעם איז זי געוווּן זיכער. ביסלעכווײַז.

זי וואָלט זיך געלערנט זוכן אין וואַלד—וועלכע יאַגדעס צו קליַבן, וועלכע אויסצומיַדן.
זי וואָלט זיך געלערנט וואָס איר קינד באַשיצן. זי וואָלט זיך איַנגעהיימישט; ווידער געזאָגט
וואָלטן זיי ביידע וואָס דאָס געטאָן. און ווען דער וואַלד וועט אָנהייבן ווערן קלענער, וואָלט זי זיך
אַריבערגעקליבן,
ווי די בערן, הירשן, און די שאָפֿן פֿאַר און זיט מיט זיט מיט איר, צוריק אין די פֿאַרשטעעט אַריַן,
זוכן מיט איר ניַ אַנגעשאַרפֿטן חוש הריח. אָבער איצט איז ניט די פּאַסיקע

Temperance Movements

Just when we learned to roam in this tongue,
to shed awareness of our tendency to round vowels,
to not round the vowels at all, to respond without pausing,
to dip into pools of colloquialisms and Technicolor slang
emerging from taverns and street corners, approved in cafés,
and ultimately sanctioned by language academies,
to enunciate with the flag aflutter (but not waving) in our larynxes,

Just when we learned the nuances of these recipes,
now is the time for the flame lowered, this will render the dough
flaky, here the garnish and there the drizzle of gravy
on flower-bordered porcelain and beneath the silverest cutlery
for framing is equally crucial all points that cannot be taught by
recipe books but only by experts schooled by forebears over fires roaring
on a day defined by sheets of rain tolling against pane and roof

Just when we learned to tailor our dress,
to don the tones of our surroundings, to relinquish the shades
of breeze fluttering palm fronds and petals, to accept instead those
of pewter and slate and coal dampened by mist, to look away from or
reach out to those who persisted in those now impossible shades, caught
in dreams that were for us becoming ever more distant in memory,
to persuade them that our way was for the best, for the now,

Just when we learned the trajectory of events foundational,
when the patriots had outlined the parameters of community, illuminating
signals in fields, sending messengers to dodge the tyrant's boot, when the
generals had released the call for the men to step away from the barley
harvest, when women were recruited for the sewing of uniforms,
nursing the wounded, and indoctrination of the young, always the young,
when the community so long imagined finally became the motherland,

Just when we had been rendered into citizens extraordinaire hewn until
pliant, and simply just here, on this divan together in this flat on a Friday
night after services and dinner, just then did the petitions begin to
circulate, and the boycotts, once dismissed as ineffectual, began to
strengthen. Far from defending us from the plans forming abroad,

our neighbors found themselves eager to learn more about
and to execute those very plans.

Only when we accepted the inevitability of the end,
only when we had confirmed that a cousin across the ocean
would indeed shoulder the burden of us, only when we had gathered
our medals and prizes for services outstanding rendered
did we pause to finger the shapes
of a collective self that we could not even begin to locate.
What for these accomodations?

In our flawless diction, we lauded the architectural intricacy of the
parliament building. We remembered X who had presented us with a then
obscure pastry when we moved into these now bare rooms. Its
sweetness reminded us of the flourishes and swirls of our (once)
parliament. We giggled despite ourselves. Gloves in hand, tremors
shielded by a black veil, Mother urged us to finish packing and to brace
ourselves for the avalanche of nostalgia sure to come.

Silent No More, or,

Notes on Melodrama Re-visited

We did not bemoan all that was unavailable to us. To what avail that?
Instead we found our way into the mode of the day. Our heroine batted
her eyelids regularly; her waist arched seductively, yet always within the
limits prescribed by the Code so that her virtue was never in question.
The villain's eyes exuded ambivalence, evil even; we were certain his
audacity would elicit shiver. For comic relief the supporting cast bumped
into each other, sending coconuts flying, glass shattering, pies splattering,
upending all of the ne'er-do-well anti-hero's well-constructed plans.
It was controlled chaos. Slapstick admittedly but given its strategic
placement, not *slapshtik*. Of that we were hopeful.

In fact, our hopes were high all around then. In the night of the cinema,
we hoped to paint escape in motion, to banish rent due looming. We
gathered weekly to compare notes at our favorite deli on the palm-lined
concourse. The food on offer was "of our people" to be sure but adapted
to the New World (and in fact would not likely have been had in the
Old One). We knew our audience: Aunt Beyle, whose child perished
at birth, who drifted from room to room in starlight; Uncle Moyshe, whose boat
never landed, who never struck gold in the Golden Land. If our convolutions
and gags smudged the circles beneath their eyes, we knew we had succeeded.
Our art sparkled crimson against disdain.

Generations after our departure, a violinist composed a score that
honored our mission. White curls waving, her accompaniment didn't
slow down our plot but revealed the deliberation that might have been if
only we had had the technology. Her notes paved an entrée into our
intention for Beyle's and Moyshe's descendants. How fortunate were our
creations to have met her melody these many years later. Somehow we no
longer had to be explained, somehow our advocates no longer had to
apologize or mention the novel we had hidden in a desk drawer or the play
we had hoped to produce in the experimental theater downtown.
Somehow our work was not *dated*. In the underworld, our skeletons
stirred, smiled; overhead, our tombstones straightened.

Varieties of Light

Billy, light in the head, light on his feet, can't help himself.
The sun flickers over his eyelids as he inhales the scent of eggs deviling.
With bass call and flick of tail the cow tickles him into her placid world.
Delighted are the squirrels when Billy releases filberts into their grip;
delighted too the reeds parted before his breathlessness
as he races to heed the bell. Delighted is Billy.

Billy, light in the head, light on his feet, can't help himself.
The equations, figures, and formulas careen just out of reach as he hears
the route to honey being mapped near the water pump in the schoolyard.
Instead of the generals and their feats he envisions the sculpting of plums,
the rounding of purple, in orchards just nine minutes away. Apples, too.
Billy, you must remember the causes and results of the Battle of X ....

Billy, light in the head, light on his feet, can't help himself.
He stops to view the progression of ants so that a sheep or two
wanders away from his fluttering fingers, his lacy whispers.
Only the vigilance of his sheepdog, long accustomed to the ways of Billy,
keeps the flock intact. Billy kisses her graying muzzle,
croons his gratitude into her tapioca fronds.

But it is at dance that Billy is most Billy. Here his lightness becomes
lightning itself. There is no dance—circle, line, pair—that eludes him.
His maiden dance partners forget their beaus, with their demands,
grateful for the respite afforded by Billy's ease. The villagers beckon
Billy to dance in the center, his eyes now slits, his face open in abandon,
their cheer separating then re-braiding the strands of his light.

Billy, light in the head, light on his feet, can't help himself.
The forearms of the visitor shimmer in the barn's flickering glow. Each
hair curling over the man's shirt is magnified to Billy's eye. Aching to
touch that hard and yet so soft skin Billy follows the visitor far out beyond
the barn into fields he never knew so distant. And it is there that Billy, his
eyes now terribly open, is discovered, under a linden tree, by a peddler.

Billy, light in the head, light on his feet, couldn't help himself.
But the villagers did try to help. They searched for clues; they set up
services and stones. Refusing all solace, his nana would have none of it.
Only at midnight does she rise from her rocking and muttering, to inscribe
the legacy of her boy, her charming Billy into dale and meadow, ever
keen to the singsong of his light visible just over the black horizon.

Dreams of Declamation: an Invitation

*(a screening of Night Train by Jerzy Kawalerowicz
at the National Gallery of Art, Washington, D.C.)*

We chat in the ancestral tongue and await the curtains parting on the film
in which, we will learn shortly, a character who eluded the tentacles of
genocide, figures peripherally but critically. The series of masterworks
from the (New) Old Country, of which this film is a part, has been curated
by an auteur known chiefly for unflinching visions of the city. We're keen
to see today's offering, and how we will be changed. The light is already
dim, a transition into the study in shadow and dark soon to unfold. We
expand into the cool of this crepuscule, vibrant with anticipation.

Suddenly a woman turns around and asks whether that's Y we're speaking.
We assure her that it is indeed, granting her the stage to launch into what
will surely follow (and does): how she was never taught Y, how her parents
spoke Y only when they didn't want her to understand, how the sounds of
Y are familiar to her, how sometimes she almost thinks she understands Y,
how she wishes Y had been taught to her, and underlying it all,
the unspoken refrain: how she really wishes it had all been different
than it was and now can never be.

And then the lights darken entirely, and we are ushered onto a train journey
dense with love impossible and ambition dashed and history unbearable.
There are so many signs at play in this claustrophobic zone moving, ever
moving. There are wheels clanging on tracks and trains coursing
through the proverbial tunnels. There are trees that flit by—pines, birches,
and those that are only whirr. And there are branches of said trees
swaying against the heavens as the perpetrator is pursued by passengers,
crushed by their zeal. And then there is the passenger, noted above,

who remembers even more crowded trains some years prior and who
warrants this second mention. And I think back now to the woman who
turned to us, like untold others, in recognition immediate but partial,
blurred really. She who sat in the dark as sounds ricocheted around her, as
she was kept apart, made to embed in not-knowing. She who reached for
sleep, tossing and turning as partial comprehension pummeled her dreams.
As she turns to us, this system of signs, at once a representation of love and
a method of exclusion, hovers in ambivalence. Instead of the film,

I turn now to her, to usher her elsewhere, to say: Perhaps this won't be
the Paradise of Knowledge envisioned as you lay rigid with fury in your

girlbed. The going will be faltering: the irrational gendering of the nouns,
the pesky adjectival endings, the word order. And the words themselves
thickened by a tongue that will (now) never be native. Yes, there were the
words of your parents and grandparents and of a ship journey in steerage
and of aunts and uncles who never did flourish; yes, symbols of not-quite-
ness, the cringe ongoing of being new and poor and still unripe, *di grine*.

Yes, but also were there words of others who chronicled dislocation, lyrics
that lead you to the time when our people formed battalions against
bloodshed and organized against injustice pervasive in ways wide-ranging
and unpredicatable, in rallies and picnics and lecture halls and reading clubs.
And sang those verses at those events so that there was no wall,
or even membrane between word and deed, song and action.
And all of this in sounds only whose outlines remain familiar.
But also you, quietly, a place for you.

For here you are in a clearing, in late morning light,
under a hat wide-brimmed and burgundy-ribboned,
in an ivory linen sundress to which a lace collar has been affixed.
And yes these details are crucial.
And here you are, I see you, as you touch that collar, as you speak,
no recite, no *declaim* words from a small journal now
no longer forgotten, words that might have been whispered to you
had fate willed it so,

had that constellation of family and history practices in that home in
Great Neck, Long Island been otherwise.
Only you have chosen them now,
have found them, in your determination,
your will to be other than the woman
who happened to hear Y spoken in a gallery auditorium
but rather one who turned to establish a way station against
history's demon of indifference.

Here is a place—an ashes-of-rose damask chaise lounge, in fact—for you.
Here, let me remove your hat;
let me bequeath you this ticket pressed between crumbling brown pages,
let me observe your travels from family to the cafés of the Marais and
Union Square and Whitechapel and then back to the front porch, only now,
your aunt and uncles (if not your parents) are beaming with pride,
let me heed your declamations of fire,
let me weave these wild flowers through your summer morning curls.

דריי איך זיך איצט אויס צו איר, אַריינצובאַלייטן אין אַן אַנדערן אָרט, צו זאָגן: אפֿשר וועט
דאָ ניט זײַן
דער גן-עדן וואָס דו האָסט אויסגעדמיונט בשעת דו ביסט געוליגן שטיקף פֿון כעס אין דײַן
מיידל-בעט. דאָס גיין וועט זײַן אין קורצע און אָפּגעהאַקטע טריט: די אומראַציאָנעלע מינים פֿון
סובסטאַנציוון,
די זלידנע אַדיעקטיוו-סופֿן, דער ווערטער-סדר. און די ווערטער אַליין
געדיכט געוואָרן אויף אַ צונג וואָס וועט (איצט) שוין קיין מאָל ניט זײַן הי-געבוירענער. יאָ, עס
זײַנען געווען די
ווערטער פֿון איערע עלטערן און באַבע-זיידעס און פֿון אַ שיפֿריזע אויפֿן צווישנדעק
און פֿון מומעס און פֿעטערס וואָס האָבן קיין מאָל ניט מצליח געווען; יאָ, סימבאָלן
פֿון ניט-אין-גאַנצן-קייט, דאָס אָנסופֿיקע מה-יפֿיתדיקע זײַן ניט און אַרעם און נאָך אַלץ
ניט-דערגיין, די גרינע.

יאָ, אָבער געווען זײַנען אויך ווערטער פֿון אַנדערע וואָס האָבן דערצייילט וועגן
פֿרעמדקייט, ליריִשע ווערטער
וואָס האָבן דיך צוריקגעפֿירט צו אַ צײַט ווען אונדזער פֿאָלק האָט געשאַפֿן באַטאַליאָנען
קעגן שפֿיכת-דמים און אָרגאַניזירט קעגן וויטגרײַעכיקן אומיושר וואָס מע האָט
ניט געקענט
פֿאַראויסזאָגן, אין מיטינגען און פֿיקניקס און לעקציעזאַלן און לייענרײַזן.
און געזונגען די סטראָפֿעס בײַ די די אונטערנעמונגען כּדי עס איז ניט געווען קיין וואַנט,
אָדער אַפֿילו היטל ניט צווישן וואָרט און טאַט, געזאַנג און טוווּנג.
און דאָס אַלץ אין קלאַנגען פֿון וועמן נאָר די קאַנטאָרן בלײַבן דיך באַקאַנט.
אָבער אויך דו, שטילערהייט, אַן אָרט אויף דיר.

ווײַל אָט ביסטו אין אַ פֿאַליאַנע, אין שפֿעט-פֿרימאָרגן-ליכט,
מיט אַ ברייט-ראַנדיקן הוט מיט ווײַן-רויטע סטענגעס,
אין אַ לײַוונטן זונקלייד ווײַס ווי העלפֿאַנדביין מיט שפֿיצן-קראַגן.
און יאָ די פֿרטים זײַנען קריטיש.
און אָט ביסטו, איך זע ווי דו רירסט אָן דעם קראָגן בשעת דו רעדסט,
נייִן, רעציטירט, ניין דעקלאַמירט ווערטער פֿון אַ זשורנאַל איצט
מער ניט פֿאַרגעסן, ווערטער וועלכע מע וואָלט דיך אפֿשר געהאַט געשושקעט
ווען דער גורל וואָלט אַזוי געוואָלט,

ווען די קאָנסטעלאַציע פֿון משפּחה און געשיכטע אין אָט דער היים אין
גרייט-נעק, לאָונג-איילענד וואָלט אַנדערש געווען.
נאָר דו האָסט זיי איצט אויסגעקליבן,
זיי געפֿונען, אין דײַן עקשנות,
דײַן ווילן צו זײַן אַנדערש פֿון דער פֿרוי
וואָס האָט צופֿעליק געהערט יי אין אַ גאַלעריע-זאַל
אָבער נישערט עמעצער וואָס האָט זיך באַשלאָסן צו עטאַבלירן אַ בנין-מיקלט אַטנקעגן
געשיכטעס שד פֿון גליטכגילט.

אָט איז אַן אָרט—אַן אַשן-פֿון-ראָזע-דאַמאַסק "שעז", טאַקע פֿאַר דיר.
נו לאָז מיך אויסטאָן דעם הוט בײַ דיר;
לאָז מיך דיר איבערגעבן בירושה דעם בילעט געקוועטשט צווישן בלעטער וואָס
ברעקלען זיך,
לאָז מיך קוקן אויף איערע נסיעות פֿון משפּחה אין די קאַפֿעען פֿונעם מאַרייַ און
יוניאָן סקווער און וויטשטשעפֿל און צוריק צו דײַן -גאַניק,
איצט, נאָר איצט, קוקן דינע מומעס און פֿעטערס (אויב ניט אַיערע עלטערן) אויף אײַך מיט נחת,
לאָז מיך זיך צוהערן צו דינע דעקלאַמאַציעס פֿון פֿײַער,
לאָז מיך אַדורכקוועבן אָט די ווילדע בלומען דורך דײַנע זומער-פֿרימאָרגנדיקע-לאָקן.

חלומות פֿון דעקלאַמאַציע: אַ פֿאַרבעטונג

(אַ וויזיונג פֿון נאַכטבאַן פֿון יערזשע קאַוואַלעראָוויטשן בײַ דער נאַציאָנאַלער-גאַלעריע,
וואַשינגטאָן, דלק)

מיר שמועסן אויפֿן אמהות-און-אָבֿות-לשון און וואָרטן אויף די פֿאַרהאַנגען זאָלן זיך עפֿענען
אויפֿן פֿילם
אין וועלכן, ווי מיר וועלן זיך באַלד דערווײַסן, אַ העלד וואָס האָט אויסגעמיטן די
פֿאַנגאַרעמס פֿון
גענאָציד, פֿיגורירט אין דער פֿעריפֿעריע אָבער בולט. די סעריע מיטסטערווערק
פֿון דער (ניו-) אַלטער-היים, פֿון וועלכן דער פֿילם איז אַ טייל, איז אָרגאַניזירט געוואָרן
פֿונעם קינסטלער באַוווסט דער עיקר פֿאַר זײַנע דרייסטע ווייזיעס פֿון דער שטאַט.
מיר האָבן חשק
צו זען דער הינטיקער שאַפֿונג, און ווי אַזוי מיר וועלן זיך בײַטן. די ליכט איז שוין
פֿינצטערלעך, אַן איבערגאַנג אַרײַן אין דער שטודיע פֿון שאַטן און פֿינצטערניש
וואָס וועט זיך באַלד צעווייקלען. מיר
ברייטערן זיך אויס אין דער קילקייט פֿונעם בין-השמשות, צאָפֿלען מיט דערוואַרטונג.

פּלוצעם דרייט זיך אויס אַ פֿרוי און פֿרעגט צי דאָס וואָס מיר רעדן איז יי.
מיר פֿאַרזיכערן זי אַז עס איז טאָקע און לאָזן זי אַריגינלאָנצירן
אין וואָס וועט זיכער קומען נאָך דעם (און קומען קומט עס טאָקע): ווי אַזוי מע האָט זי קיין מאָל ניט
געלערנט קיין יי, ווי אַזוי אירע עלטערן האָבן גערעדט יי נאָר ווען זיי האָבן געוואָלט אַז זי זאָל ניט
פֿאַרשטיין, ווי אַזוי די קלאַנגען פֿון יי
זיינען איר באַקאַנט, ווי זי טראַכט אַז אָט-אָט פֿאַרשטייט זי יי,
הלוואַי וואָלט מען זי געלערנט יי, און אונטער אַלץ,
דער ניט-דערזאָגטער רעפֿרען: ווי זי וואָלט טאָקע געוואָלט אַז אַלץ זאָל האָבן געווען אַנדערש
ווי ס'איז געווען און איצט קען שוין קיין מאָל ניט זײַן.

און נאָכדעם זיינען די ליכט אין גאַנצן אויסגעלאָשן געוואָרן, און מע האָט אונדז
אַריבעגאַלייט אויף אַן באַן-רײזע
געדיכט מיט ליבע אומימגליכלעך און אַמביציע צשמעעטערט און געשיכטע ניט איבערצוטראַגן.
פֿאַראַן אַזוי פֿיל שילדן צו דעשיפֿרירן אין דער קלאָוסטראָפֿאָבישער זאָנע זיך באַוועגנדיק,
תּמיד זיך באַוועגנדיק. פֿאַראַן דאָס קלאַפּן פֿון רעדער אויף רעלסן, און די באַנען וואָס לויפֿן
דורך די גוט-באַקאַנטע טונעלן. פֿאַראַן בײַמער וואָס לויפֿן פֿאַרבײַ—סאָסנעס, בערעזעס,
און די וואָס זיינען נאָר אַ פֿלעק. און פֿאַראַן צווײַגן פֿון אָט די בײַמער וואָס
שאָקלען אַנטקעגן די הימלען בשעת דער פֿאַרברעכער איז זיך נאָכגעיאָגט פֿון די פֿאַסאַזשירן,
צעשמעטערט פֿון זייער קנאָות. און פֿאַראַן דער פֿאַסאַזשיר, שוין אויבן דערמאָנט,

וואָס געדענקט אַפֿילו מער-געפֿאַקטע באַנען מיט אַ פֿופֿצן יאָר פֿריער
און פֿאַרדינט אָט די צוווייטע דערמאָנונג. און איך דערמאָן זיך איצט אין דער פֿרוי וואָס האָט
זיך אויסגעדרייט צו אונדז, אַזוי ווי אָן אַ שיעור אַנדערע, אין תּיכּפֿדיקער אָבער
טיילווייזער אַנערקענונג
נעפֿלדיק, דעם אמת געזאָגט. זי וואָס איז געזאָען אין פֿינצטערניש בשעת קלאַנגען
שפּרינגען אָפֿ אַרום איר, בשעת
מע האָט זי געהאַלטן באַזונדער, געהיטן זי זאָל בלײַבן אין ניט-וויסן. זי וואָס האָט זיך
גערייכט נאָך שלאָף,
דרייענדיק זיך אַהין און צוריק בשעת טיילוויזיקע פֿאַרשטענדניש צעשלאָגט אירע חלומות.
ווען זי דרייט צו אונדז צו אויס הויערט אין דער לופֿטן די סימנים-סיסטעם, אין
איין וועגס אַ רעפּרעזענטאַציע פֿון ליבשאַפֿט און
אַ מעטאָדע פֿון אויסשליסונג, אַפֿילו מער ווי דער פֿילם אַליין,

Fellowship Prize(d)

Once I knew buses,
I could tell you the path of the cross-town 33, past the grocery
on the corner of X and Y, where I would descend, with my shopping cart
clattering behind me, and enter the realm of the divine.
Here, spices, greens, fish, meats would elicit a reaction Pavlovian in
regularity. I knew I would unlock the mysteries of this bounty.
Salvatore (I could never bring myself to call him Sal) would croon the
discoveries of the day and offer a wink and a special discount.
"I take good care of you," Salvatore said. And so he did.

Once I knew buses,
I could tell you the path of the 41, how it stopped at the overpass, you
know the one, where honeysuckle twinkles with such insistence. On the
promenade, Ethel would tell of what ought not be missed at the
Cinematheque. Irving would regale with tales of nude beaches of yore.
Betty would point out the flight of birds only she could spot. Even without
binoculars Betty knew. Only Leo couldn't bring himself to merry. Ethel
did so try to extricate him from the nightmare ongoing that began with
a knock on the door so long ago. Still, Leo never missed our Fridays.

Once I knew buses,
I could tell you the path of the 107, with Mr. Jackson (I never knew his
first name) at the helm for at least 16 years. I remember the day he started.
How Delia always knew where to get the best orthopedic shoes. She had
to, with all the trudging over marble and mahogany she did with a vacuum
cleaner and mops and such. How Esperanza favored the 8:23 bus, with
her kids to get to school and so many errands to run. It was a good
time slot for her, for us all. Reasonable. Mr. Jackson always said to me,
"Don't get into no trouble today, hear?" when I departed his 107 bus.

Only now I know these walls.
It's my arthritis, my circulation, and my heart. It's almost everything
really. Salvatore's market is long gone, replaced by a liquor store, with
deals struck out front at all hours of day and night. Salvatore would be
distraught. Ethel and the Promenade Gang have all passed. I won't go
into the details, except to say that Leo outlived them all. Except for me,

of course. The 107 route was discontinued. I tried to find out what
happened to Mr. Jackson, but got nowhere.
They said they didn't know of a Mr. Jackson.

Only now I know these walls.
And I was never much for decorating. Just didn't have the knack. But
always were flowers. Now Esperanza walks up the three flights to be
with me. She arranges for groceries to be delivered.
She brings me flowers; she opens the windows for me
so that I may smell that which I can no longer see. Esperanza remains
to me from the buses that zigzagged across the avenues and boulevards of
the metropolis scarred by potholes never repaired (despite my pleas),
through the honking of cabbies and the swerve of bike messengers,

past ladies stepping over puddles and excrement,
beneath the awning of live oaks whose lowermost branches caressed the
bus roof at Eighth Avenue and 13th Street as the "Stop Requested" bell
chimed in our ears. Esperanza remains to me from the buses that
delivered me to and from the central municipal offices those many years.
Once I knew buses, once I knew buses. Now Esperanza washes me,
now Esperanza holds me, now Esperanza sings to me melodies of her
abuela, as geraniums and daisies and poppies (and what's that other one)
sway nearby, as these walls inch ever in.

From Night to Night

They said he was asexual. His gaze was downward.
The herringbone pattern of the brick sidewalks occupied his mind's eye.
He tried to find a formula, the key to its geometric order.
And then too were the weeds flourishing between the bricks,
eluding the death-tug of the upkeep man hired by the
civic-minded citizens, the promoters of beautification.
Only he found pleasure below in the shapes of weed green,
in their purple and yellow flowers resistant to footsteps.
And when weeds were absent, he imagined their flourishing,
as if planted and tended. *Did anyone plant weeds*, he wondered.
And thus in the downward pull of his gaze they said he was asexual.

They said he was asexual. His gait was methodical.
He measured his steps, savoring the movement of the mechanism that was he,
the miracle that rendered his limbs obedient to his commands, an obedience
absent from the body of his sister Sheyndl, whom he wheeled everywhere,
not to stares, but to uncertainty and grim cordiality. Sheyndl's
determination necessarily propels this poem. And he appreciated too the
shapes of their bodies through space, how space never seemed negative.
Even when Sheyndl wasn't with him, he considered how the spokes
of her chair wheels would gleam on a particular day, for example,
on this silver Sunday in the park by the Soldiers' Memorial.
And thus in the method of his gait they said he was asexual.

They said he was asexual. His grin was partial.
It was noted in photographs how he never fully smiled,
as if the constellations of sadness in the world and in his life
prevented a full range of horizontal mouth motion.
Still there was the fullness of his lips—luscious, someone once said;
strawberry smoothie at an August picnic, another opined.
Strangers tried to realize the potential of that fullness
with antics and tomfoolery; acquaintances knew otherwise.
Even when he thought he had mastered a grin in completion,
he was informed by others that, in fact, this was not the case.
And thus in the partiality of his grin they said he was asexual.

They said he was asexual. His days were full.
He reshelved books at the public library. Fiction was his favorite,
but he loved too biographies and historical monographs, the lives of others.
He was always happy to substitute for the children's librarian
when she was out. Story time was never a burden, for he always knew
which book to select, the words right for the day. And the sonorousness
of his voice transfixed the children, rendering them reluctant to leave.
But eventually they did, knowing he would surely be there next time.
He was always there, as he was almost never sick, the children observed.
Their parents nodded, reflecting inevitably (and silently) on his asexuality.
And thus in the fullness of his days they said he was asexual.

They said he was asexual. His nights were turbulent.
After he fed Sheyndl, after they recited the *Shema* kneaded into them by
their widowed mother decades ago, after he lifted Sheyndl from her chair
and into bed, after he fell under the covers, memory wielded power.
Specific fragments: weight above rendering him immobile,
breath volcanic in his ear, and pain beyond words. And so he turned
to the owl hooting in the forest, alert to the creatures below
scurrying in the undergrowth, to the medley of cricket song,
to the thrum and reverberation that was the village night
that would shepherd him slowly, patiently from that night long ago
to the one night now shakily at hand.

～ II ～

LIFE STUDIES IN YELLOW

AND OTHER PRIMARY COLORS

Movement, in Black and White

The photograph finds you so.
A tendril or two have escaped your cornflower-bordered kerchief.
You sit on the back stoop of a rowhouse; an air conditioner protrudes
from the kitchen window. A child's arm reaches forever across your lap.
There is a particular model of car in the left-hand corner that scatters
grains of bitterness onto this genealogical moment.
You are looking away into action occurring beyond the frame.

There are children whose games hover on the brink of quarrel.
There is a husband whose underwear will soon need placement on the line.
You try to remember the whereabouts of clothes pins.
There are dresses that require mending, although your own
on this day drapes elegantly over your crossed legs.
All of this is somehow apparent from the trajectory of certain lines around
your turned-away mouth, certain etchings in your turned-away brow.

And from hands, mapped by calluses and veins, that even in stillness,
seem without rest, searching for signposts, en route to the next task.
These are hands that have learned to improvise, to conjure, to repair.
They are rarely without food or utensil or article of clothing.
And so the still hands, or rather the still itself,
becomes a film viewed, a moving picture as they say,
whirring quietly in the cinema of memory.

Except your eyes. Only these are off limits.
Perhaps it is the angle of the camera, the photographer racing to capture
what we may never know. Perhaps it is the guarding of self,
the retreat of the subject: *not me, surely not me. Here are these others.*
Mother, there is no need to look at the camera.
Even caught unawares, you are prepared.
Even in contour and still I see you.

Where Once Were Cherry Blossoms

You should have come in spring.
A light translucent scalloped the noonday lake.
The water tranquil pummeled the barricades of our winterness.
Coy fish caressed our limbs free of care.
Brightly, we drifted on seagrass gondolas.
The echoes of anise arias trilled from weeping willows onshore.
Nymphs arrived to usher in the season of dance.

You should have come in spring.
Fragrances leaped from the hearth over flagstones onto the village green.
Perhaps of mimosa or peppermint. Perhaps of purple pears?
Loaves laced with crunch and cliffs lined sideboards and tables alike.
Intoxicated, we nibbled on bliss morsels until the moon slipped away.
The poor came to partake.
And still there was more.

You should have come in spring.
We walked the meadows glistening; hope we chanted into rain:
Esperanza! Esperanza! To farmers we called out silkily of harvests
to come and the gilding of tomorrows. We spooned gnarled oaks;
eagerly, we embraced branches discarded over lanes once impassable.
We dozed under the crackling of crows; the gaze of the jackal could not
diminish our gratitude. Our barn doors were ajar.

You should have come in spring.
Then you could have floated with us, then you could have dined with us,
then you could have rejoiced with us.
Now you have arrived, stumbling, into an era of whispers and weeping,
with its tangle of gray,
its residue of accusation.
Now look how you have landed into the epicenter of emptiness.

If you had heeded our call, you would have seen Mother descend
the staircase with her smile and her symphony.
You would have felt her touch, papery with purpose.
You would have felt her kiss against the remnants of your sorrow.
Come you instead to this bed, with its whiteness so fleeting and these
whimpers emanating from depths we could never have foreseen.
Come offer witness to the fruit of your delay.

Radio Nights in Candyland

How Mother did love melody—
in spite of herself, in spite of prohibitions, Mother floated on rhythm.
Sometimes on the stoop at eventide, her mother's hand skimming, leaving
flour dust in her braids (so that Mother had premonitions of an
old age that was never to be hers), sometimes skipping down the street,
sometimes in the technicolor gloom of her father's grocery store, her
fingers drifting to the jar of licorice, sometimes in the weeds beneath the
bridge, releasing fireflies into blues, snippets from the wireless
would send her foot tapping, her skirts flying, her soul dancing.
Little girl Mother came to understand swing.

How Mother did love song—
she seemed to know them all. Ballads, commercial jingles, labor songs,
love (requited and otherwise) songs, lullabies, patriotic songs were
absorbed. As the Sabbath Queen was welcomed, as the men praised
the Woman of Valor, Mother accepted Bing's invitation to join him in
his hit of the day. Of course he could depend on her to know the song;
of course she joined him, again despite the prohibition.
How could she refuse Bing? In the turmoil of the marital bed, in
the gray of the sun intervening, Mother reached for these sweetmeats, for
only their lusciousness could still the trembling of her hands.

How Mother did love her stories—
the trysts between doctors and nurses, doctors and patients,
administrators and … transfixed Mother. The bouts of amnesia, the legal
battles, the rescues from storm embodied the possibilities of both focus
and flight. Forbidden from viewing the airbrushed faces and sculpted
bodies on the filth box, Mother improvised instead with radio.
There, she quickly recognized voice and inflection and
slights barely veiled by dialogue peppered by pregnant pauses.
Anchored in expertise, Mother became a prophet of plot prediction,
a scholar in praise of the implausible.

How Mother did love art—
words arranged, distilled into alchemy. In all our together years Mother
never attended a concert, never visited a cabaret or dined at a supper club,
never sought an autograph, never stood onstage herself. Yet sometimes,

in just such a setting, when I spot woman alone at a table with orchid, connected to the singer by an elemental force, I am certain it is Mother. Only I face instead a woman on her knees over the kitchen floor tiles, varicose-veined legs extended from housecoat, gladdened momentarily by the sounds above, or hunched over a stationary bike, pedaling against sugar rising, ever rising, to a compromise that can never be.

Diabetic's Fantasia

In dream was candy sanctioned, encouraged even. Candy of all sorts.
For the chocolate lovers, there were pralines, nougats, truffles, and
bonbons. For others, there were brittles, caramels, licorice,
jelly beans, mints, rock candy, sourballs, taffies, and toffees.
All these, to name but a few.
The sheer variety was on an unprecedented scale, far beyond the halls
of candy we had experienced on trips to the Continent or the teeming
confectionaries off the alleys in regions yet further afield.

Youth, whose whiteness of teeth was rivaled by the whiteness of their lab
coats, proffered these delicacies with smiling indifference. There were no
inquiries into our medical history, no question of whether we had funds or
insurance. We were here to partake. This was the proverbial candy store
of our childhood; only we now had the discernment to truly savor
its nuances. We reached out to accept with newfound abandon,
dispelling the anxiety that had come recently to define us.
Finger-pricking instruments were on hand. Just in case.

The tastes were of course also unprecedented. We could
detect layers of flavor; a complexity of the highest order. We could
isolate strands of hazelnut prancing through truffle, mint veins
extended through chocolate rendered buoyant by the freshest milk.
We could trace the interconnectedness of each element,
the lacework of it all. And we did see them as elements, not merely
ingredients. Perhaps we would need lab coats of our own?
Our exclamations murmured through the echoing marble aisles.

We were the opposite of Lucy and Ethel in the chocolate factory. There
was no binging, no fear of being caught, for as was suggested earlier,
there was no question of wrongdoing. Far from it. Our doctors, at
the marble-topped tables, smiled at us in approval. Or at least that was
how we interpreted their smiles. Still, we noticed they were merely
onlookers. We wondered what they were writing in their notebooks. We
noted suddenly the absence of cakes and cookies. Our calm began to
dissipate. Slowly, we drifted from delirium; slowly, we groped for insulin.

Rope as Instrument of Liberation

The young daffodil loved to jump rope.
He found an ease in the skip, a synchronicity in time with twine.
The girls on the playground invited him to join;
there was something infectious about his fleetness of foot,
never fancy, never trying to impress,
but always steady, joyous in the relief of partaking.
Even when he tired finally, stepping on the rope,
he was happy to take his turn turning,
content to encourage,
respectful not to look below skirts
occasionally arisen or awhirl in wind.

And it was just that ease that proved his downfall.
None of the girls exactly wanted him to look up their skirts,
but they thought it odd that he wasn't at all curious,
like other boys. He even seemed to look away when
their flowered underpants flashed into view.
However, this looking away couldn't save him.
Little girls' underwear was not to be *considered* by little boys,
even if only to look away and even little boys shaped like a daffodil.
And suddenly the girls' daffodil, once a mascot, became a target.
And he was encouraged to drift away from little girls, and so he did.

And the daffodil did find companionship in the company of another,
who although not a daffodil, was similarly betrayed by a lack of
coordination and anxiety resultant from a nose that was always running,
and the two spun stories of the most improbable sort, having to do
with the adventures of Marcel, a French spy, who was really spying for
Russia since France was an ally, until the daffodil's companion was called
away, drawn by the siren call of belonging among boys more … boyish.
And so the daffodil followed. But so hopeless where their passing skills,
so slippery their hands around a football, so inept their swings,
so wild their throws, it seemed that all was for naught.

They were both invariably selected last; the teams would always
divide them up: "You take the daffodil; we'll take the other."
And still they persevered. His friend improved somewhat;

the daffodil never did. Once, he astonished all by making a spectacular
catch; another time, by slamming the ball beyond the diamond,
perilously close to the church beyond. But these were the exceptions.
Despite his persistence, despite the relative lack of jeer,
all the daffodil wanted was to return to the rope and the girls.
Only it was too late, of course. And so briefly the daffodil jumped rope
with his sister and her friends in the driveway at home.

And when it was too late for that,
he would take the rope out late at night,
when mother was asleep, and father was at study in the front room,
and he would skip down the streets, with the whirr of bats overhead
and the furtive but determined transit of raccoons alongside, with the
necking and heavy petting going on in unlit cars and arguments visible
between the parted curtains of kitchen windows that little daffodils were
not supposed to witness, and he would jump *thumpety-thump* but with the
dexterity for which he had been known. The raccoons peered out from
behind trash bins, their masks crinkled in merriment.

Flower Moon Dress

On the sweatshop floor, in the din of many machines,
the young daffodil was confronted by a panorama of paucity.
There were blues, blacks, grays, browns, and tans, but little else.
The daffodil was not surprised,
for this was all that was acceptable and in fact all he had
ever seen worn by men and boys in his short life.
Yet somehow he could not believe this was to be his fate every Sabbath,
every holiday, and every occasion from here on out.
He who had worn colors of a wider sort,
foresaw a future of somberness unfurling before him
and looked to the exits and the grated windows for escape.
But his father's hand was firm around his,
and the little daffodil was pulled along into the abyss of absence.

The daffodil was no stranger, even at this young age, to dislocation.
Already, he had been told that he must accompany
his father and brothers to Sabbath services.
Hitherto he had basked in the sweep of his mother's arms
as she prepared to recite the blessings of the Sabbath candles.
This was the true origin of the Sabbath, not when the men and boys would
welcome the Sabbath Queen in song hours later. *This* was when She
arrived. The little daffodil had seen the Queen step over the threshold,
had seen Her accompany his mother to the couch in rest,
had seen Her welcome the neighbor ladies to his mother's living room
as they discussed the events of the week and patted his head,
as he moved between their work-swollen hands.
He had touched the miracle of the onset of rest.

And even amidst this lack, the daffodil, given the smallness of his frame,
had fewer options still. Of this, father and daffodil were informed,
as the clerk quickly eyeballed the daffodil.
Of course, they could select a larger suit,
but alterations would cost more and result in delay.
Father was not pleased at either of those possibilities. And so the daffodil
was made to thrust his stalks into navy blue pants and jacket and was
appalled at the plainness of the color, the dullness of the cut,

the lack of luxury that was its polyester fabric. Daffodils are bright yellow
and should never be thrust into navy blue. He knew this even then.
However, the suit met the father's approval,
and the two exited the factory sewing room floor.
A future of daffodilian drabness had commenced.

But the daffodil proved worthy of the reputed resourcefulness of his kind.
It may only be March, but a daffodil must march forward.
With his face and body still hairless,
the daffodil found ease in skirts and dresses,
the ideal mannequin for his sister's sartorial explorations.
With her he could explore an unlimited array of color,
lavenders, pinks, greens, especially seafoam—
the daffodil rejoiced in them all.
He paraded up and down the floor of their bedroom
or that of their playroom near the attic and saw himself
as the matriarch who did not have to go off to services on Friday,
who could host the neighbor ladies and exchange anecdotes.

How he envied his sister,
who could enjoy these fashion options at any time,
who did not have to depart the warmth of the Sabbath home.
His sister, stung by the exclusion from services
and the study of certain texts, chuckled mirthlessly at his envy,
"Silly daffodil! and then prophetically:
"You won't feel this way years from now."
The daffodil could not then imagine years from now.
He was merely glad to find now respite, however brief,
from the void of navy blue and such.
He smiled quietly, enigmatically even, at his sister's words,
adjusting the waist of his pink flowered dress in the meanwhile.

The Weeping of the Willowy,

or,

Why the Daffodil Did Not Become a Drag Queen

As his skin was invaded by hair with a fervor ferocious,
faster than the German invasion of Czechoslovakia and Poland,
faster than the Soviet invasion of Hungary
and yes also Czechoslovakia,
spreading over his chest, face, stalks, and even back,
all once smooth and gleaming,
smoothly gleaming,
gleamingly smooth,
transforming the willowy into the furry,
as if a fur coat erroneously arrived from Macy's
had been set upon him and could not be removed or returned
as stated in not so small print in the terms of purchase,

As the hair proved surprisingly adaptable, settling in for the long haul,
getting *rooted*, as it were, in the hospitable terrain of his pubescence,
as the daffodil found it increasingly difficult to ascend to the playroom,
to hide the effects of this invasion from his sister,
as their play became increasingly strained, for turning his back
was no longer enough, for the tufts rose above his undershirt
and winked out from its short sleeves,
as the dresses of which he had been so fond,
and which had, truth be told, suited him so,
began to look less organic, less unforced,
although not entirely devoid of a certain charm,
his sister and he admitted,

As it became increasingly fraught for them to fashion this into fashion,
as the dresses outgrown by his sister were folded and packed away,
the daffodil had to bid farewell to this period of guarded play,
had to face, truly face, the fact that long masses of upswept curls or
the simplicity of a bob would never be options for him,
that the vision of himself as the perfect *baleboste*, renowned not only
for her household skills, but for the modest elegance of her person,

as wife and mother and grace incarnate—
the ultimate *eyshes khayel*—would never come to pass,
as the daffodil had to face the terror and emptiness of that loss,
had to weep unconsoled before the mirror,
for his sister was away at dodgeball practice,

As the daffodil told himself that this life,
actualized with the sponsorship and protection of his sister,
had finally come, clunkety-clunk, to an end,
that he could no longer be the exemplar, he briefly considered
the role of fashion consultant to his mother and his sister and friends,
but they made it clear that such counsel was not sought,
and so the daffodil, accustomed to a life of circumnavigation,
withdrew still further within, for all around him were young men
suddenly taking shape, with shoulders broadening, voices deepening,
arms thickening, and yes, with hair that seemed so suitable for *them*,
and as he could not retreat to a playroom to hide their effect on him,
the daffodil knelt down and prayed for a patch of earth there his yellow
bulb to shine.

baleboste (Yiddish, of Hebrew origin): housekeeper, housewife
(also landlady, hostess)
eyshes khayel (Yiddish, of Hebrew origin): woman of valor

Midnight in the Garden of Gridiron

The daffodil finds himself called to the gridiron long past the call to sleep.
He walks to a nearby school, as his yeshiva lacks such facilities.
There are few athletes in the yeshiva, and even the most gifted
among them do not focus on the training needed to excel.
Matters of the spirit necessarily take precedence there;
the body is a vessel that allows the soul to flourish.
And yet this lack of athletic super-prowess at his yeshiva has not
diminished the daffodil's sense of inadequacy on its fields, although
perhaps it has lessened the taunts, which truth be told, are not as frequent
as they might have been elsewhere, for example, at this nearby school.

He is not surprised to find the field gates ajar,
for he has absorbed early that access can be denied
even without barking dogs or sirens or locked gates, for that matter.
He sashays down the sidelines, taking in the sweep of the field,
the panorama of its enormity, challenging for the most disciplined of
athletes, let alone a daffodil under powerful, if partially lit, floodlights.
The bleachers are empty, but he can perceive the cheers
that so often flooded the streets on Friday nights,
when the Sabbath, with its rest and quiet,
commenced for the daffodil and his folk.

In this quiet, the daffodil can make out the shapes of the bodies
hammered into strength and speed straining against tight shiny jerseys,
the grunts of their forward thrust. He wishes not to be of them really,
but to be the one for one of them,
to feel strong arms around his impossibly willowy stalks.
He can't imagine how of any of this can happen;
and even as a young daffodil, can't see how it ever will.
Still this dream, this image really, for nothing ever happens
beyond the envelopment of arms, the embrace ultimate,
flits through his fevered mind as he continues to make his way downfield.

The cheerleaders are no less present than the objects of their cheer.
The daffodil is dazzled by the lustrousness of their hair, apparent even in
ponytail and so different from his own sidelocks and shorn skull.

And the uniforms, with their bold lettering and skirts so skimpy
to reveal bodies lithe and proud. And why shouldn't they be proud?
He would be too if they would let him be one of them.
Even he has to giggle at this incongruity,
for what place a daffodil among cultivated hibiscus?
The symmetry of the chants and cheers eggs him on in delight,
and the daffodil is now past mid-field.

The play in this world just beyond his cloistered one has influenced him
more than he's been aware, the daffodil perceives. The style and stakes
and structures here have determined the fate of his bloom. But tonight he
is not concerned with difference or apartness, call it what you will.
Instead, the daffodil begins to dance just before the end zone.
It is a dance of simplicity and charm, with the understatement of the
moderns and the ardor of the ancients. It is the ultimate solo act,
of course, with none to join, and none even to witness.
This is his touchdown. Here, tonight, his skirts skirting cleated astroturf,
the daffodil finally touches down.

The Devil Behind the Details

The daffodil was not known as a master of the Talmud.
In vain did he venture into the whirlpool of argumentation.
He toiled to keep track of all of the variables such as
the condition of the cow gored by the ox,
the circumstances (and permutations thereof) of objects lost and found,
the height required for the walls of the harvest festival huts
all of the details fueling the commentators,
generations therein and thereof. This was the zenith of learning
treasured in his community. This was what was extolled
on the streets and in the houses of study and the folk literature
and in the logs and ledgers of the marriage brokers.

And it so happened that several centuries before the daffodil's arrival
there was a movement reacting against this very casuistry,
one led by a charismatic figure who called for simplicity in all things
and walks into the forest, to commune with the natural world,
with its creatures of all sorts and sizes,
and with *Got der Bashefer*, the Creator of them all,
to listen closely to their sounds and songs
and the daffodil might have flourished in this movement,
with its simplicity, but the daffodil was not born into this movement
and in any case long before the daffodil's arrival the movement
had spun webs of strictures and restrictions of its own.

And although, with his diligence and intermittent infatuation
with the elegance of the abstraction if not the details,
the daffodil did get by on the talmudic byways,
generally making grade and (barely) passing muster
and sometimes on good days even achieving excellence,
the title of master was never within reach.
For the daffodil was happiest with his novels,
with their characters and dreams of escape not unlike his own,
and with his walks in the parks, especially the one with the
footbridge which required leaping from stone to stone,
leaping, that is for one as small as the daffodil.

And though the daffodil thought he was coming in below
the radar, doing just enough to avoid a lashing of belt and tongue,
this was not the case at all.
In fact, he was quite above said radar,
given the prominence of his father in that school,
and given his own engagement with godless learning,
which was admittedly required by the godless state,
and at which the daffodil quite thoroughly excelled.
And so it seemed that he was applying himself further to one
body of learning—an impure one—at the expense
of the other—the holy and true one.

And so the daffodil had to be sent away, banished
to a citadel of learning, one seemingly more worldly,
where he might better absorb the habits of holiness.
Only other events were to occur to the daffodil,
ones that left him reeling,
retreating further away, away to he knew not where,
praying nightly for emancipation,
even a return to the school from which he'd been banished,
with its asceticism and purity, where his star had not been stellar
but had at least been faintly visible (with a telescope)
in the tangle of talmudic argumentation.

Daffodil in Danger

In his new yeshiva, the site of his banishment, at which the daffodil was
to imbibe the ways of the sacred, in an atmosphere supposedly less
cloistered, the daffodil did not fare well. Here, in contrast to his previous
yeshiva, the reputation of his father—saintly, learned—carried less weight.
Although it did grant him entry into an advanced class without an
entrance exam, the name of the patriarch could not protect him from the
onslaught to come. The daffodil did make do with his unremarkable
talmudic study, trying to deflect attention. Only now were added the
burden of Torah study, and the daffodil and his classmates had to
memorize verses of the weekly portion and the insights of the
commentator Rashi. And the daffodil's equilibrium, a rather delicate
contraption under the best of conditions, began to fray.

His daffodil-ness, noted in his previous yeshiva, was now veritably neon.
He did not halt the downward trail of his wrists, the mince of his step,
the sweep of his daffodilian appendages. And while there had been
handsome young men in his previous yeshiva, their sober garb and
scholarly mien, not to mention his own retreat homeward after studies,
had not led to explosions in daffodilian lust.
All of that changed now.
The daffodil was surrounded by young men, in less theological clothing,
which did nothing to disguise bodies lithe or muscular or strapping,
shoulders broad, forearms rippling, biceps so bulging.
There were young men outstanding in athletics,
football and baseball to name but a few.

And the daffodil had to dorm with these strong young men,
with bodies so different from his own. And he did encounter them
shirtless en route to the bathroom or naked before the shower
or in conversation with the bedroom room door ajar
and his gaze lingered where it was not permitted,
and his hands strayed too long in his pockets.
And although he never approached any of these young men
or even sought their attention so total was his fear,
retribution was swift for the daffodil. And the daffodil was hunted,
not for the prize of his yellow brightness,

but for the twin transgressions of his daffodilian self
and the desire which seemed to fairly crackle from his fragile frame.

And the daffodil was captured and driven into rooms on the verge of
violet by bruise, and kicks were aimed against his form,
and punches and slaps did soon follow,
and lo in vain did the daffodil seek to avoid said blows.
Huddle and hunch and fetal position were all to no avail.
For the blows were applied with precision,
and the daffodil, with his whimsy and dreaminess,
was no match for the speed and skill of his tormentors.
And the daffodil's stem was crumpled, and his petals battered,
and his bulb lost its light, which may have been attributed
to the change in season or location or simply not noticed at all,
for no one in authority ever sought to address the situation.

And in vain did the daffodil seek to flee his tormentors
for they always knew where to find him, how to corner him,
how to force him into dark rooms with corners cavernous
that seemed never to end, as if utterly removed from a world
the daffodil, in his naivete, had imagined to be civilized,
not to mention sacred.
And the daffodil, who had been plagued by terror and anxiety
generated by his daffodil-hood,
became a jangle of nerves,
unable to sleep, always running,
trying to be present and absent simultaneously,
the walking ghost of legend.

He struggled to master the schedules of his tormentors
so as they not to face,
but here too the daffodil was no match.
For they changed their schedules frequently
and always knew where to find him in order
to inflict ample torment but never to mangle
or uproot the daffodil altogether
from this garden so very far from Eden.
And if this poem seems to have no conclusion,
that is how the days of the Reign of Terror were experienced
by the daffodil. And thus shall this poem come abruptly
and without grace to a halt.

Disciples of Dorothy

At the end of the summer following the Reign of Terror,
dread suffused the daffodil.
His body started to tremble and his stem to shiver,
and how the daffodil did weep, pleading hysterically
(as he would not do again until a certain night years later)
that he not be made to return to the yeshiva to which he'd
been banished and face the next phase of the Reign of Terror.
And his father was consumed by consternation, for if the daffodil
had to leave this yeshiva, which was after all, somwhat modern,
where would the daffodil go? The options that would meet
the father's standards of respectability were dwindling indeed.
What would become of the daffodil?

And the trembling that had begun at the thought of return
transformed into full-fledge swaying without stop.
But his father insisted,
and thus was the daffodil boxed and shipped back.
And the daffodil had nowhere to turn,
no soil in which to anchor his buffeted roots. Only his father had a plan
of his own and wielded his influence and made some phone calls and
said the daffodil never knew what. And it was made clear that the
daffodil was off limits, could not be brutalized,
and the daffodil was thus saved by his father—sort of—
since it was his father, after all, who had sent
him (and bade him return) to the scene of his torment.

And the daffodil had to face again those tormentors,
who never referred to the past.
It was as if none of it had happened,
or as if it had been erased.
As if it could be erased.
Poof (ter) indeed!
And the daffodil did adjust,
although this erasure left him unsteady on the ground,
not knowing whether the torment would begin anew,
even as he was grateful for getting through each day

without the choreography of kicks, the plethora of punches,
the tango of thrashing.

And the daffodil did find roommates, who provided camaraderie just
within the margins. One had memorized the works of Gilbert & Sullivan,
corresponding even with the D'Oyly Carte Opera Company, and here
the daffodil first encountered satire and silliness with a purpose
interpreted by the ladies Parsons and Ronstadt, among others.
And another was a refugee from a country commandeered
by the faith police, having fled the homeland
of which his ancestors had been for centuries a part
and arrived with his brother
at this yeshiva to which the daffodil had been banished.
And there was another student, who was insightful and elusive
and provided pleasant conversation for the daffodil.

And thus did the daffodil find a place to regain some brightness,
and there were empathic teachers, too,
of religious and general studies alike.
One of the former met with him to discuss matters of the spirit,
and even though the daffodil never did reveal his daffodil-ness
or discuss it with this rabbi,
the conversation and care and time did buoy his day.
And the daffodil was encouraged too by one of the latter,
who in his obesity
and with the insight of the outsider teaching literature
in a setting where it was little valued,
saw in the daffodil some of his own outsiderness and love of language.

And in time did the daffodil turn somehow
to the writings of Dorothy Parker. Dorothy *Rothschild* Parker.
In her stories of women waiting or spurned,
in her poems and sayings,
in her reviews and commitment to the art of words,
in her macbre book titles,
at the round table at which she presided with other luminaries,
the arbiters of literary and theatrical taste,
in her political commitments and the blacklist,
he found wit and courage and determination and action

infused with an understanding of loneliness and melancholy,
a kindred spirit of sorts.

And although the daffodil knew even then
that he would never preside over such a table
trading barbs and bon mots as elegant as the hotel surroundings,
given his diffident daffodilian self,
her writing and example transported him
from a constellation of violence and silence,
to another in which a daffodil could find a way
and perhaps some day even flourish.
And thus the daffodil, while staying afloat in the Talmud and the Torah,
did bury himself in her writings and her example
and did traipse to different libraries to uncover articles and books
and all of this in the years before the internet.

And the daffodil did write a very long paper on Dorothy P.,
who like his father, ended up being a savior of sorts.
And later he did discover her favor among other daffodils,
and was glad to have known of her in his youth,
when he was young and lost and terrified,
and glad too to return to her years later.
And even though one of his brothers would observe to another
that the daffodil had been changed forever by the Reign of Terror,
that his bulb was never as bright,
and his light was never as unwavering,
the daffodil would remain ever grateful for the shelter
he found amongst Dorothy P. and her kind.

Candy Tattoo

Never get into a car with strangers.
Beware of the temptations they may offer,
Mother warned, then burning to her theme:
they may beckon with treats, ones you know to be sanctioned,
such as those from Paskesz or Goldenberg's dark chocolate peanut chews.
They may even appear to be members of our community,
alluring in modest garb. They may even call you by your name,
but if you don't know who they are, do not get into the car.
Do you understand? Show me you understand. Good. Still not entirely
satisfied, Mother would return, trembling, to the concoction
at hand. For now, let us say barley soup or brisket or …

Would that I had heeded those Mother words.
Of the many proscriptions to which we were tethered, this one evoked not
merely sin or stain but danger. We who were showered with eggs and
tomatoes from university dorm rooms, we who were hounded en route
to school (even when we thought we knew which streets to bypass),
we who knew to travel in packs, we were no strangers to danger.
Yet this was different. Perhaps it was the pairing of strangers with candy,
the notes of terror flecked throughout the sweet familiar.
Perhaps it was the entering into car, the being whisked into gone-ness.
There was no proliferation of photos on kosher milk cartons back then.
But somehow we knew.

Would that I had heeded those Mother words.
There were other rooms I might have entered on that brink-of-autumn
night, such as a coffeehouse on the avenue, redolent with bean,
purring with machine and the strumming of guitar. Or a back room,
darkened perhaps, but governed by restraint. But alas such rooms
were not selected that night. Instead, after disembarking a crosstown bus,
another room, tucked between warehouses, proved irresistible. Here,
TV screens flickered above ballads of lost love lament drifted through
Marlboro mist men slouched in corners with booze and/or smoke in
hand observing assessing nodding turning away gazing then staring
returning until finally he approached a mask of scruff and blur

his torch alighted upon me could it be yes he was upon me and was now whispering candy words nuzzling them into my neck etching them into skin where they emblazoned their intention with a singularity of purpose so that the ballads the smoke the touch which should have been enough for now for this first encounter only they weren't and so I devoured the candy a glutton became I mistaking sugar for care following outdoors his broad back t-shirt loose over his belt the clomp of feet on pavement into the car gleaming inscrutable so that those Mother words were not forgotten or discarded even but overruled so that I glimpsed Mother in glint after the lighting of Sabbath candles in anticipation of rest as the youngest born to her near middle age glided into catastrophe

Two Men Outside the Mirror's Frame

He might have come to me sanctioned by a matchmaker, who considered
his attributes and how they might complement my own and mitigate those
features of mine less … complimentary. She would have consulted with
her colleagues, the rabbinical ladies congregated between the lighting of
the Sabbath candles and the chanting of the ode to the women of valor.
She would not have needed a ledger, like the one she had in the office in
the back of her shop. In matters of the heart, the matchmaker's mind, or
rather her intuition, was legendary.

The matchmaker might have touted her hypothesis in its formative stages
to test it upon the other ladies, assessing its feasibility and impact,
by the nodding of wigged heads,
by the width of eyes narrowed in candlelight,
by the enthusiasm of clucking,
and the tenor of the debate ensuing, skills unmatched by their fathers
and husbands and sons and uncles and nephews in the houses of study.

He might have come to me blessed by a friend who recalled me at a party,
at which innumerable eligibles were assembled. She who delighted in
such gatherings—in the pouring and imbibing of spirit, in the trading of
tidbit on the doling of fellowship and prize, in the glide across dance floor
between swag and bodies ever changing, in the exchange of liquid
permitted amongst such august revellers—always kept me in mind.
In the gusto of potion in goblet, she would have conjured me.

For such gatherings were terrifying to me, not to the I that might have
been, but to the I that was, the I who scrutinized bi-lingual dictionaries
and pondered the nuances of words across language, the I who
could not conceive the steps needed to command this friend's poise
and occupy her stilettoes, or even to be rooted as self amongst selves,
the I who huddled at home and wondered
if the word "snogging" could ever again be au courant.

He might have wooed me with words not of promise of fortune
or holidays in Tuscany or Oaxaca or Eilat or the end of struggle with
the arbiters of fate, the monarchs of the minute magazines, but rather of

encouragement on the necessity of art despite hunger and obscurity and
rejection and censorship and indifference, and of titles read and savored,
not only those from bright young things whose flame was snuffed out
meteoric, but those from the enduring and the endurers.

He might have kissed me gently on lips never before kissed,
teased his tongue over the lines of my jaw and the nape of my neck,
as I luxuriated in the size of his hands caressing the swell of
cheeks as my legs opened in welcome.
He might have been any of those
men doing any such so.
Only he wasn't. And he didn't.

There was no matchmaker,
no keeper of accounts.
There was no kissing.
There was no teasing.
There was no gentleness.
His hands, though large, did not caress.
And my legs did not remain open in welcome.

And thus do I rummage,
in pallor of day and impossibility of night,
through the shards of counter-history, still glittering despite the years,
to locate him beyond shadow,
to topple him from the pedestal of Might-Have and
to instate in his rightful place the Gentleman Caller closing the front gate
and strolling now, past the camellias, up the garden path towards me.

First Fruit (and Aftermath)

How is it I glimpse you at moments unforeseen and now suddenly often
fleeting you flit through my neon nights and zombie days
you whose name I may never have known whose features are a blur
as I replay crystalline the absence of words in the car
on the way to the other side, your fist at ease over the stick shift
the knots beginning to coalesce in my belly's basement

so that scouring the dishes in the latter day
the steel wool begins to fray
my hands start to chatter
I have to set down a Fire King cup seafoam spinning
clutch the rim of the sink
steadied somehow by asterisks of steel wool drifting across worn steel

how is it that I remember instead pain searing altogether unprecedented
the bludgeoning of desire into ashes the blossoms ripped scattered
the cherry tossed into garbage etc. etc. without ado without letup
despite screams severed at the mouth imploring derailed
weeping to no avail surely a body cannot withstand this
wondering is this where it all ends just as it is beginning

so that nearly a quarter of a century later
I still flinch at touch unexpected, resist the call to remain,
flee repeatedly as if to banish that moment when I failed to flee
could not dislodge the tonnage, the force that had discovered me
the ingénue in the shadows who had mustered late the courage
to sit at the soda fountain counter of breathtaking fulfillment

how is it that one night gone very awry is accorded so much sway
it ought not be so it could have been so much worse after all
why pen these words for such things are surely best left … only here they
are, these words that necessarily approximate, inevitably fall short into
hodgepodge, lead me to pause the record so scratchy, to find the flashlight,
to part the cobwebs, to never locate you wherever you may be, to stagger
towards letting go

ביכורים (אָדער נאָכווירק)

ווי קען עס זײַן אַז איך אַז כאַפּ אויף דיר אין מאָמענטן ניט־פֿאַראויסגעזעענע אַ בליק
און איצט פּלוצעם אָפֿטמאָל
פֿאַביגייענדיק שוועבסטו אַדורך מײַנע נעאָנע־נעכט און זאַמבי־טעג
דיך וועמענס נאָמען איך האָב אפֿשר קיין מאָל ניט געקענט וועמענס שטריכן זײַנען
צעשוווומען
אַנשטאָט שפּיל איך ווידער קרישטאָליק דאָס פֿעלן פֿון ווערטער אינעם אויטאָ
אויפֿן וועג צו יענער זײַט, דײַן פֿויסט געמיטלעך אויפֿן אויטאָ־שטעקן
די קנופֿן אָנהייבנדיק זיך פֿאַרמירן אין מײַן בויקס קעלער

אַז דאָס אויסשיערן די כלים
צעדריבלט זיך די שטאָל־וואָל
צעפֿלאַפֿלען זיך די הענט
מוז איך אַנידערשטעלן אַ "פּיעער־קינג" טעפל דער ים שוימיק דרייעניש
כאַפֿן דעם אָפּגאָס קאַנט
געפֿעסטיקט ווי עס זאָל ניט זײַן פֿון שטערנדלעך שטאָל־וואָל וואָס שוועבן אַריבער אָפֿגעניצטן שטאָל

ווי איז עס אַז אַנשטאָט געדענק איך פֿײַן זודיק הייס סך הכל אומגעוויינטלעך
דאָס צעשמעטערן תּאווה אויף אַש די קוווייטן צעריסן צעשיט
די קאַרש אַרײַנגעוואָרפֿן אין מיסט אַרײַן וכו' וכו' אָן פֿאַנפֿאַר אָן אויפֿהער
ניט געקוקט אויף געשרייען אָפּגעשניטענע בײַם מויל דאָס בעטן רחמים אַראָפּגעלאָזט פֿון די רעלסן
דאָס ווײַנען אומזיסט אויף זיכער קען אַ גוף דאָס ניט פֿאַרטראָגן
זיך ווונדערן צי עס האַלט זיך בײַם סוף גלײַך ווען עס הייבט זיך אָן

אַז שפּעטער מיט אַ פֿערטל יאָרהונדערט
דערשרעק איך זיך בײַם אומגעריכטן אָנריר, שטעל זיך אַנטקעגן דעם רוף צו פֿאַרבלײַבן,
אַנטלויף כסדר אַזוי ווי צו פֿאַרשיקן דעם מאָמענט וועלן ס'איז מיר ניט גערעכט אַנטלויפֿן
ניט געקענט אַראָפּוואַרפֿן פֿון זי די מאַסע, דעם כּוח וואָס האָט מיך געפֿונען
די אַנזשעניוּ אין די שאָטנס וואָס האָט זיך שפּעט געספּראָוועט צום מוט
זיך צו זעצן בײַם סאָדאָ טאָמבאַנק פֿון ווונדערלעכער אויספֿאַלגונג

ווי איז עס אַז אײַן נאַכט אַזוי פֿאַרקריִמט געוואָרן באַקומט אַזוי פֿיל דעה
ס'דאַרף ניט זײַן אַזוי זײַן ס'האָט דאָך געקענט זײַן אַזויפֿיל ערגער
צו וואָס פֿאַרשרײַבן די דאָזיקע ווערטער ווײַל פֿון אַזעלכס איז בעסער ניט ... נאָר
אָט זײַנען די דאָזיקע ווערטער וואָס געוויס זײַנען בערכדיק, אומפֿאַרמײַדלעך ניט גענוג,
דאַרפֿן זײַן איבעגעראַרבעט, פֿירן מיך איבערצורעוויזן דעם דיסק דעם פֿיל צעקראַצטן
פֿונאַנדערצוטיילן די שפּינוועבס, דיך קיין מאָל ניט צו געפֿינען ווּהין דו זאָלסט ניט זײַן, זיך צו באַרען
פֿאַמעלעכדיקערהייט אויף אָפּצולאָזן

Trimming, Then Watering the Flower

The daffodil cannot bear to bare his back.
Covered in waves of fur flourishing, seemingly relentless,
he curses anew the irony of a daffodil's back being thus coated
and shivers in shame at the thought of its exposure.
And here, no less, in this, the capital of the land of his forebears, a city
venerated for the crumbling elegance and curvilinearity of its buildings,
the brilliance of its pastry, and now, at hand, its legendary bathhouses.
Having come all this way, having vowed to partake of the waters,
the daffodil must be trimmed. And so the daffodil's companion,
or horticulturalist as it were, applied the lotion to the back in question.

And in this act did the horticulturalist reveal her dedication.
What a gardener wouldn't do for a daffodil!, she commented wryly.
For the odor was most unpleasant, neither herbal nor medicinal,
but reeking somehow of desperation, which is never pleasant to behold,
even to an advocate for daffodils. And although she did inwardly wince,
the defoliation was completed, to the satisfaction of the daffodil and
to her expressed disappointment. For she preferred a daffodil in its natural
state, and thought such lotions the height of folly and self-loathing.
The daffodil did not necessarily disagree, but the stares and the
sidelong glances, even of strangers, were too much to be countenanced.

And so the daffodil emerged with his shorn (if reddened) back
into the pools and whirlpools of various temperatures, drifted into the
liquid currents, and paddled through the passages of pleasure, eyes barely
conscious of others around him, for boundary itself had become fluid.
He heard exclamations of delight, and words in the local tongue and his
own and many others, and floated along on this raft of word and water.
And in this reverie did he migrate into the interior of the baths,
through the reflections of others flitting through marble columns,
against mosaics, into waters placid under a dome
and murmuring rendered resonant by echo and sunbeam and splash.

And from there he moved to dry wood, where forms of all sorts
were on display close at hand—the lithe, the muscular, the obese,
the aging, the drooping—

and of course fur inevitably in patches, in waves,
but also in patterns unexpected—
here a horizon, there a pinwheel—
all these forms crammed in a space so narrow
and yet the breathing was even
and the bodies were observed but accepted,
or at least not remarked upon,

And in any case, he couldn't speak the local tongue,
and there appeared to be no one to translate,
despite the assurances that everyone spoke the international lingua franca,
only they did not.
Of course, they did not.
But no matter, for here was the daffodil, clipped, watered,
illuminated now not by almost-moonlight but by incandescence
and dry heat, perspiring onto wood,
his skin expanding with (and into) that of these others,
at one with the Danube night.

A Knight Shining, Without Armor

As the years did pass so the daffodil did cobble together a survival of sorts.
He buried deep his secrets, and endeavored to forget them.
And to reify their remove, to seal their coffin, as it were, so that the
secrets would never reemerge or be faced and so that the events hidden
would not reoccur, the daffodil commenced a new project.
His daffodildom had to be overcome to maximize his survival chances.
In other words, rather than cultivate his inner daffodil, he worked to
extinguish it. And the daffodil did go to the gym and did lift heavy
weights and did study the techniques of lifting in bodybuilding
manuals and he did overload his body with fuel to feed his ever growing
muscles and to bury still further the unspeakability of himself.
And lo was the daffodil transformed into a tank.

And as a tank he did garner glances glad returned on the street
and in the bathhouses and in the kudzu-choked expanses
behind the city park. And the daffodil did find connection,
however fleeting, in this semi-public erotic sphere.
And here he would kiss strangers in the day and in the night
and run his hands over them and entwine himself with them and
sink to his knees and perform that which shall not be named in this poem
for the daffodil does not wish to offend his more modest readers.
And on his knees, with his mouth full, so to speak, the daffodil did pray
that the police would not arrest him for indecency or worse and that he
would not be pummeled and left to rot, for kudzu is rapacious and would
quickly cover the remains of a daffodil, even one transformed into a tank.

And as risky as was his activity—the groping and stroking and beyond—
at least there were others around, and the daffodil thought that perhaps
this was safer than going into a car and entering an apartment where he
would meet a fate even worse than the one met on the night so terrible
that it had to be buried and there would be no one around to witness
or help just as there had been no one on said night.
And the daffodil did encounter others truly interested
in more than an encounter of the byway. Only they did grow
impatient for there was much that the daffodil could not bear
and ever did the daffodil deflect and pirouette so as not to
reveal and not to face his secrets. And these others left him to his dance
steps and his evasions, however inadvertent they might have been.

And the daffodil did so yearn for someone less readily deflected.
And he would dream of this figure, as if in daguerrotype, as someone
strong and gentle and patient, someone who would button the
button on the back of his shirt collar in the morning as a gesture
of good tiding for the day and then nuzzle his neck and give his ass
a squeeze as he raced to catch the train. And after yet another
needle-in-the-haystack online date, the daffodil would think of the knight
while staggering towards sleep, this knight on a white steed galloping
towards the jumble of bramble and thorn and kudzu and muscle that
formed the daffodil's carapace. And thus did the daffodil's years pass,
with secrets intact and glances returned (or not) and beds briefly shared
(but mostly empty) and hooves of the knight's steed always within earshot.

To the Boathouse

He said, "Past the park." And then: "Through the gates. No code needed.
The end of the drive, upstairs." I made my way down the boulevard,
with its tree canopy and mansions of architectural interest,
so aware of this configuration of green, these circular drives,
these intricate gates that directions had not been needed.
The door was of course ajar. I had come to him.

At first I couldn't detect him in the gloom, despite the spartan
surroundings. But there he was, in a gray linen shirt and pants of
uncertain hue and fabric. In dusk, he appeared little changed.
Graceful even in repose; flurries sprinkled amidst gold.
I had expected photographs (of the son at least) and, from the rumors,
paraphernalia or, at least evidence, however barely apparent.

But there was nothing, only his sleeved arms around my quickly naked
self. And his tongue whispering words of such hunger that I must surely
be hallucinating, drifting, reverting back to seminars skipped on the
Peloponnesian War and Orpheus descending ever descending, so as not to
miss a moment of this golden skin stretched over limbs and Adam's apple,
risking, but ultimately avoiding expulsion not for knowledge unmastered

but for duty unmet, laughingly if casually celebrated
in the glitter of summer holiday, the lushness of lazy days on the lake
with other (golden) apples and bodies dappled by radiance
refracted through the tops of birches, racing through
ferns and earth dense with kisses unending, unexhausting,
without need then for words, as if finally outside language itself.

And then the ensuing decades, the grind of making-do.
The fruit of my conscientiousness and diligence, the scholarship student
rewarded by a post, a cubicle in the dungeon, far beyond the marble
corridors, sorting, selecting, safeguarding brittle volumes. And the nights
in small rooms, themselves adorned by later editions of some of the
aforementioned volumes, hoarding remembrances of that time,

my summer sojourn in the understated world of the half of one percent,
where he moved so effortlessly, so tenuously until these years later, back
again, observes wryly, "Not so much exile, but the periphery of things."
And then: "When will I get my act together?" I grope for
a witticism about acting and togetherness, and find instead
his dry cheeks, his now trembling hands.

Portrait of a Predecessor

I.

His photograph stands to the side of your (our?) bed.
Occasionally, when my eyes wander during love,
when I am lost in my greed for you,
when I have to turn from the ever expanding boundaries of said greed,
when I am inside you, savoring the gift of you, confident of the now,
but knowing this can be withheld or removed altogether,
I glimpse him.
There he is, handsome in a patrician way.
Is that unoriginal? Perhaps, but "objectively" stated, there it is.
Standing against a tree of a species indeterminate (to me),
he looks outward, away from you.

And yes, I still see the pull of him, not just in his looking-away-ness.
I imagine—for you won't provide the circumstances—
you snapping this photograph strategically, for the camera is steady
and the image is crisp in black and white.
And I imagine you in the pre-digital days,
in the red of the dark room,
your excitement, the image unfolding from chemicals,
the precision of framing, the symmetry of composition,
the presentation of a man whose lines and angles,
whose ambivalence about privilege and his own survival seems
perfectly suited to that backdrop of tree in that late afternoon light.

And I see you choosing the frame for this image,
a plain black one with the narrowest of ivory inlay,
and I see you taking the framed photograph with you on each of your
many moves, wrapping it in tissue paper, and then in bubble wrap,
laying it atop the mounds of peanuts, and then once unpacked,
selecting the suitable place of honor in the new abode:
not the den, not the living room, but the bedroom.
We bring our histories with us; our skeletons usher in our days.
And so I give welcome to this man, this third wheel, or should I say
fifth column. I bid him stay, here with us in the open, astride our love,
and I reach for your waist, as you moan in memory lost to me.

II.

His portrait stands above my bed, my north star.
His wisdom, his play, even under duress, still surge
though the march of the just-this-side-of-chaos that is my life.
And yet when I am with you, when I feel your weight above and within,
it is you who are foregrounded—the direction of your touch, the hunger of
your hands and lips and tongue and cock, all of you, the ways our bodies
seem to know each other and to find yet surprise. And yes, they often
spoke of his background—the stone mansions set back in woodland,
the yachts glittering on turquoise, the schooling in those many countries,
etc. And yes, that may have been a draw in the beginning, for how could
it not be, given my yeshiva origins, but it did not remain so for long.

For on that day in woodland more modest, he revealed otherwise, and that
is what called me to stay. There, over my offerings of a white fish salad
and bagels picnic, he found the words to convey horrors of which I cannot
even in this poem write. He so feared the weight of these revelations,
how they would flatten the most buoyant of afternoons like this one,
or worse surely, our nights of entwinement. And so to assure him that they
would not, we documented the day. In his looking slightly away from the
camera after we, quickly, even haphazardly, found a pine against which to
pose him, there was such a tenderness, such a hope for our togetherness
that I felt reassured, did not need to dash to the dark room.
The photograph would emerge when ready; there was no call to rush.

I recall happening upon the frame in an antiques mall off the interstate,
when I was looking for a gift for him.
There it was just beyond the carnival glass and art pottery,
as if someone had decided against its purchase at the last moment.
And I knew immediately that this would be the one to shield that day.
And when I moved those many times, trying to flee the loss of his
optimism, the loss of rootedness, finally the loss of his self,
I would never pack him away in bubble wrap, sealed and inaccessible,
but would keep him with me, in my "carry-on" or "carry-with"
not as shrine or talisman or guest
but as part. And so here he remains
beside us, beside this bed, which I hope will long remain ours.

Through a Lens Shuttered

You had traveled south to visit a friend's daughter in rehab and yet you
found a path to me. It was good to be with you, after all this time,
even if only fleetingly across a table in the central train station,
surrounded by the din of fast food consumption,
although neither of us were fast and neither of us consumed.

It was good to hear your voice, after all this time, however unsettling the
topics of your conversation: the marshaling of equanimity to face the
likely guillotine at work, the restlessness to relocate to another city,
one less brutal, where gangs of youth did not knock unconscious
lone commuters at bus stops, where night pedestrians were not accosted,

where a woman would not be attacked at the entrance to her apartment
building and then savaged in her own home, to another city
not of nightmare, wherever it may be. In short, the love fraternal in the
city for which it is renowned had not yet found you. Despite
the occasion of the visit, despite the dread delineated in chat,

it was good to see you, after all this time, to see your eyes so blue,
to see the hurricane of hair on forearms (that once encircled mine)
still brown in contrast to your beard now further flecked with gray,
to hear your voice even and steady in concern,
to know your own health was stable, despite scares of recent years.

And yet I, ever the chronicler, the archivist, meticulous with evidence
and minutes of meetings did not capture an image of this rendezvous.
Yes, the possibility of a selfie—beneath the kiosk
sign or against the stone arches—arose but was ultimately discarded
or rather relinquished. Instead, after your departure,

I exited into the station's arcade, deserted save a young
man whistling a so familiar tune that I could not name but wished to
for it might have helped explain the day and then he responded
"Christ our Lord" and I thought "Well, that's why" and I thanked him
for his melody and was glad for having heard, glad for having asked

and I continued on across the street through a grove deserted save a tribe
of pigeons resting and cooing (snoozing and snoring?) in shade canopy,
into a snow of blossoms whose pinkness enveloped me,
over a carpet of fallen fruit that bade me slow my step. Until I paused
on the stairs devoid of monument but replete somehow with homage.

And there I uncovered the return route to good, to your voice in the cosmic
cupboard where connection defies categorization, where there can be no
finding aid. Here, text messages cannot be deleted. Here, there is, if not a
lightness of being, then a more-than-bearable accretion of sun and memory
and care siphoned into silt to be stored and mined at a moment opportune.

On this day a photo briefly considered was not taken. But still are these
words, ones that number not a thousand, but honor instead a journey to
call upon the ailing, a dream of a city without savagery, a hymn whistled
above the clatter of trains, the serenity of urban birds ever underfoot,
ever on the move, a bond that is best left unnamed.

Feline Phantasm in the Midnight Forest

Despite the boxy leather couch, the oversized shaggy pillows,
the sage green walls with the almost-midnight blue accent wall,
and the parquet floors, the room seemed spartan. He would sink into
the couch, gaze into its severity, and conjure a forest at night,
then Hansel and Gretel trying to find their way home. And then he would
envision the women who landed on the foundational couches of Middle
Europe in rooms dense with learned articles and angst, so different
from this one. Sometimes he would see flickering candlelight. Or was it
gaslight? Anything to avoid the unspeakability of his long-ago.

And in just one of these evasion sessions, ensnared in a snarl of fairy tale
and Freud, he saw her. She entered stage right from the antechamber, a
queen of the realm. Her silver fur was posh (on par with the pillows),
undulating around a lithe frame. Violet eyes appeared to miss little.
Her nose twitched, sensing surely the charge in the room
wrought by horror kept in abeyance these many years.
She was not pleased by the untidiness all around.
She leaped onto the windowsill to gaze outwards,
whiskers silhouetted in the haze of almost-history.

And she stayed on that windowsill, her back mostly set against his words
ricocheting throughout the room. Occasionally, she would turn her head
to measure the pauses and the silences, blinking quizzically at the
contortions of these excavations. Her body maintained its tautness;
long did she remain in a crouch, but one ill at ease with the panorama
of blankness in front and the watchful audience behind.
Clearly, his words were diminishing the plushness of her pursuit.
There was nothing in her demeanor that invited overture.
And yet that is what he sought strangely, completely.

He envisioned her relinquishing her mission, stepping over to the sofa
and into his lap, so that his hands could unwring themselves and delve
into the rise and fall of her warmth. He didn't want to remove her from
her calling—her prey and such; he only wanted her to be with him on
this couch. She would be neither talisman nor fetish object, but rather a
source of solidarity, ushering his buried remembrances above ground.

Slowly, he would solidify the path only suggested by the found atlas.
His failure to weep into the arch of her back
would be replaced by the thrum of her purring.

But, of course, this hunter, with her blend of wild and domesticity,
did not, could not exist here. Too many are allergic to her kind.
And her presence could prove distracting, unsettling even,
given the states of duress found here. And so she had to depart
even before arrival. She did pause en route to her exit
(stage right again), her eyes meeting his, in sympathy yes, but clearly
already focused on other matters. He waved, admittedly absurdly,
at her retreating rump. Pines rustled against sage walls.
Stars drifted across now midnight blue dreamlands.

Naming without Ceremony

By now, dear reader, you might well have wondered why the daffodil
has been called the daffodil throughout this book.
You might be thinking it's time you were informed of the cause.
You assume that you have that right, given the time you've put in
to read the daffodil's own tale
as well as the tales emanating from the daffodil's meanderings of pen,
or word processor, as it were.
And you are right, dear reader.
It *is* time for just such a revelation,
or explication of this name that is not a label.

For there was available to the daffodil a wide range of name options.
And the daffodil himself did consider many of them.
They drifted through his petals, and he sojourned with each.
Unlike a tattoo etched into body, this would be a link with the soul.
And yes, a name may be changed,
but not without cost and effort and not without leaving trace.
Besides, how often do we get to select our own names?
And these were but some of the names given to those of his kind
that the daffodil did consider as he perused reference resources
of the language in which he so savored exploration:

auntie Belle Betty broken wrist buttercup daffodil Daisy

Dinah	faggot
flamer	flit
Mary	mince
Nellie	pansy
queer	sissy
sister	swish
pole smoker	prissy
pussy boy	queen
lilac	limp wrist
ginger beer	(abbr.: ginger)
(variation: fag)	fairy
poofter	(or: poof)
Molly	nancy boy
(variations:	Miss Nancy, Nance, Nancy)

And there were yet so many more, not exactly beyond the scope
of this poem, but unnecessary to transcribe here for the reader can
readily peruse such dictionaries and lexicons and the like.
This list is to give those unaware of you but a taste
of the obsession that the daffodil's kind has historically generated.
And his "taking time with each" invariably included an enunciation,
a squeezing, a rolling around in the hay of the word,
and it was far from an easy decision, given the sheer variety
and excellence of options. But the daffodil did have to choose.
And this is how a decision he did reach.

He considered the daffodil's role as harbinger,
as herald of spring, as the earliest announcement of the green-to-come,
the pioneers braving the cold and commuters hurrying by who didn't
appreciate the daffodil as daffodil but only for its role as harbinger
and despite the false starts of spring the daffodil did remain (out!) in the
cold and he thought of the bright monochrome of the daffodil, its signature
yellow, not morphed into other shades and hues to be paraded
at flower shows in order to win prizes or to attract tourists from abroad.
And yes, qualities such as hardiness, determination, foresight, humility,
visibility were certainly all qualities to which the daffodil did aspire.

But of course these weren't the sole reasons for the daffodil's choice.
Like so many of you, he had read the poem in primary school,
and with him these years the poem did surely remain. And he thought of
the loneliness of that poet by the lakes rejoicing in the expanse of the
daffodils "fluttering and dancing in the breeze" and he wished for himself
that daily reminder that though others have garnered greater acclaim for
beauty and refinement and nuance and delicacy, the daffodil need not be
retiring and he wished for himself both flutter
and dance in the breeze and the lifting of melancholy
of which the poet by the lake so long ago bespoke.

Pearl

He cannot recall the origins of his collection. There was never an
"a-ha" moment. The collected did not serve as signifiers of, for example,
a memory treasured of Mother arranging flowers before Sabbath
or of his beloved entering the door of their home, flowers in hand.
In fact, Mother often bemoaned the lack of flowers received, and he, well
he, had never shared a home with a beloved, flower-bearing or otherwise.
Perhaps you are thinking that it is this very absence that fuels his passion.
Perhaps. Or perhaps not all. Difficult to say.
We would hate to fuel empty speculation, given its abundance elsewhere.

Collecting takes him near and far. You might be tempted to consider him
an addict acting out of compulsion, as such language is rampant in the
popular discourse. But this is in fact not so, for he acts with both speed
and deliberation. Wherever he travels, he always manages to locate the
shops off the alleys, often without signage of any kind. How they remain
in operation remains a mystery to him, but not one he cares to solve. He is
content to finger the objects, careful to avoid the proprietor's watchful,
sometimes disapproving eye, scanning for marks and provenance but more
importantly for vision, for a touch wrought into spectacular—a line,
a flourish, a skein of jade.

And on those rare occasions of acquisition he never haggles. Not because
he considers it beneath his dignity. Not because he has cash to spare, for
he does not. And he knows enough about the marketplace, or rather the
shadow world occupied by others whose passion is as focused as his own,
to know when he is being swindled. Rather, he thinks it unworthy of these
objects, of the firms that took pride in this work, of the artists who labored
with love. And he does insist on words such as "art" and "artists," for
surely work that seeks to adorn and bring beauty is no less worthy
of such a designation than work that does not? And yes, *love* too.

Once, in a moment of reinvention, he removed from his apartment nearly
all of his books, the fruit of decades of browsing through second-hand
shops. A hundred boxes were carted away to a dealer with warehouses
off the interstate. He only kept books about collecting. Friends had urged
him to reconsider; the thought of his home without books was more than

they could bear. They found it anti-intellectual, self-hating even. But he
was determined, and this purge was as considered as the purchases
described above. By now you may have guessed that these "objects" are
in fact pottery, consisting largely of vases, bowls, occasionally, a pitcher.

And it is these objects that now line shelves rendered bookless.
Created for purposes utilitarian, they glow in vibrant emptiness, echoes
of life past emanating from them. Sometimes he sees his great-aunt
placing plums in a seafoam green bowl that matches one of her favorite
summer dresses. But amidst the riot of color there is one vase that always
catches his eye. It is only six inches tall, unmarked, cream colored,
with a rim that opens into petals. Arguably modest.
He caresses it as he walks by. Other than a dusting, he never cleans it.
Its matte milkiness is self-regenerating.

Was it simply mass-produced without the collector in mind?
Did the artist forget or choose to omit her signature?
What could possibly (have) fit within its narrow confines?
He knows that he will not investigate further, whether in the virtual world
or by bringing it to an auction or a dealer. And he doesn't dread what he
suspects to be an origin of mass production. He simply wishes to leave
it be, anonymous in its flower-less radiance, as he luxuriates in
a kind of not-knowing, which is a state not at all like ignorance,
but rather one that, mildly, discreetly, approaches transcendence.

The Best Let Sleeping Dogs Lie Poem

You knew there had to be a poem on this theme.
You've been asking for it all along, for these latest offerings
are excessive, even for you, mischief maker and provocateur that you are,
and even for us, the enlightened literary public.
Their subject matter may be acceptable,
perhaps even necessary, for you as fodder
for conversation in the confines of the therapist's office
or amongst close friends, but not here. We don't need or want to know.
We are sorry for you, dear flower, but your tale of woe is best left off
the computer screen, let alone the printed page, and out of the public eye.

You knew there had to be a poem on this theme.
You've been asking for it all along, for this is all too lurid, even for you.
It's akin to what one might find flipping through the channels
in late afternoon when laid low with the flu or playing hooky.
There will be seen tears, shown in close-up, the host leaning in,
with tissues at hand or on a blond end table just outside the frame,
and a studio audience in hushed sympathy followed by applause on cue
from the technicians until (finally!) the cut to commercial.
Would that there were such relief here too!

You knew there had to be a poem on this theme.
You've been asking for it all along, for all of this is disingenuous, even for you.
It would have been different if you had written a memoir, slim perhaps
but suggestive. There you could have expounded on the specifics
of your ordeal(s), given space for the grief
of the daffodil and reaction of readers.
And who exactly is this daffodil? How shall we find our footing
in this swamp between autobiography and fiction?
If you're going to come out, you can't hide behind a flower.

You knew there had to be a poem on this theme.
You've been asking for it all along, for all of this is unnecessary, even for you.
We didn't want to say anything; we hoped we could ignore "particular" poems,
But too much of this book falls into that category.
And you won't allow us to turn away. Of course we can simply close
this book largely unread, but we have chosen to respond to your work.
And don't think you've exonerated yourself by displaying this poem.
You have not. You should have known better. We're still appalled.

Memorandum to the Young Homosexual

I've seen you looking, boy.
No, of course not at an old queen like me, my southerly titties
sheathed in silk and sequins and Turkish cigarette smoke.
Still, I do have my admirers, even if you won't find them
in the bars or the bathhouses or the brambles. We gather in my apartment
well east of Tompkins Square Park. Jimmy, Stephen, Reginald always
come. Henry and Lars, too. Good men all, though not without their
foibles. Stephen, for example, has always been paranoid. Still
fearful of arrest. Yes, even in my apartment. Even to this day. I know
it's a bit out of the way, but the invitation is always open. Although the
refreshment is light—wine, cheese, crackers— and the attire is casual, it is
still a royal court of sorts. All right, a salon then, if you insist.
Or perhaps an oral history archive or a museum of relics?

I've seen you looking, boy.
It takes one to know one, and I know that of which I speak.
In my day, you see, interfacing wasn't virtual.
Encounter required touch. And to make that happen, the body and its
language had to be read, a literacy which required years for mastery.
There was nothing instinctive or "gut" about it.
The stakes were high, mind you. You could end up in handcuffs—
and I don't mean the velvet ones—in a cell with pimps and killers
and with your name on a list in the papers and out of a job.
You could end up pummeled or slashed or slain and dumped
into the river or beneath an overpass, the traffic whirring overhead—
the stuff of pulp novels minus the campy covers or noir
without the hard-nosed dick to rescue you. Of course, you still could.

I've seen you looking, boy.
I know of the gaze drawn to strapping workmen.
Sometimes I saw them on the way to my office job,
shirtless at a building site, whistling at women going by,
eating a sandwich in wax paper and swilling I-never-knew-what
from a blue metal thermos. I still recall that shade of blue.
Sometimes in the diner Helena, my girlfriend from the office,
and I favored for lunch. Their pastrami sandwiches were legendary.

No, Helena was not my beard. She was a friend, a worksite-specific one,
to be sure. Sometimes I would see men by the piers at night or early
morning, when the ache got the better of me and repartee and bourbon
were no longer enough. My reading skills were most essential
in the darkest dark, without aid of moon or flash- or streetlight.

I've seen you looking, boy.
And I am not impressed; you have much to learn.
You need to master the art of the surreptitious glance.
The eye should lightly graze; avoid the full-fronted stare,
but don't assume a position of coyness, either.
You aren't a demure maiden or a geisha.
Don't conceal your smile by your hand or shadow.
Your shoulders should not slouch,
but they needn't be militarily set back, either.
You will have to do all this in a matter of seconds. Little thing like you,
your life may depend on it. And no, that's not hyperbole.
Is there a Helena in your life? Come to our next gathering, sweet pea.
I'm sure Lars can rustle up just the right young lady for you.

Cave of Cold Comfort

I wish I could say you will grow accustomed to it,
that the jeering, sometimes blatant as from a circle in the schoolyard,
sometimes whispered as through a pile of textbooks,
will come to diminish in sting,
that you will forget or at least move on,
that you won't come to hear it even when you're in the library,
that you will accept quiet at face value and not as respite
or as concealment of said jeering about to recommence
from behind the stacks of the biology section.

I wish I could say you will wear them as badges of honor,
that the kicks and the bruises and punches and slaps
will be endured and then tended to at home in whatever way possible as
wounds of war, as if you had participated in the Battle of Bull Run or
Fallujah or somehow survived dazed (but intact) a bombing en route to
visiting an elderly colleague in a tiny country in the eye of the world's
tempest and that you won't feel the imperative to mask these badges
discovering the advantages of long sleeve shirts even in the heat
and undressing, always, always, in the beam of fog and gloom.

I wish I could say there is an inherent wisdom
to be extricated from these experiences,
that suffering ennobles or expands even,
that that which develops in the thereafter
may seem puny in comparison
but can certainly be met with equanimity,
given the extent and duration of the suffering
and the courage you've worked so hard to construct
and the perspective and distance you now presumably possess.

I wish I could say there is liberation in revelation,
that somehow these events molded into narrative and shared
will lose (at least some of) their luridness, their banality,
their capacity to burden and shame and incapacitate and render
immobile. That the action of and the agency in narration
will lift you from purgatory days in bed on a brilliant weekend,

with apple blossoms on breeze ruffling lace curtains,
that gray will transition, however slowly, into cerulean.
And that you will be en/lightened in the process.

Of course, we know that my wishes will not make it so.
But know too that even if I cannot ensure the fruition of these wishes,
neither can nor will I will them away.
For there is generosity in this goal and majesty in the mythology.
Embrace the migraine of memory. Even if only at 2:59 p.m. in the
droop of middle afternoon. Stride slowly down the stairs.
Fixate not on the proverbial light at the end of the tunnel,
but be aware of the tunnel itself, of the clamminess of its walls not
yet closing in, of the sureness of your step on stone.

And then pause for a moment. Perhaps there is a light at the end;
perhaps there is not. Perhaps there's a lantern here, where you now stand,
alongside this baggage, or rather, accompaniment.
Here is music recommended by a favorite teacher of yours;
these are passages you analyzed together after class, shortly before you
were cornered and pummeled. Here is an anthem of the birds of eventide;
these notes you learned to decipher in the forest of your own migration.
And here is my hand, chapped, veined, rough, atremble, for you to take,
as we stagger to oases obscure to our eye, past the rustling of bats
and bears and beneath the drip-drop of icicles just beginning to melt.

Night Train Over the Potomac

After a marathon day of viewing the antics and escapades,
the changes in the mores of the bourgeoisie before The Great War
wrought by an American entrepreneur
refracted through the lens (and metaphor) of shopping
as imagined for an audience delighted by the seriality of things,
after reflecting upon the publication histories of Dickens
and the brothers Singer (I.B. and I.J.)
and how prime-time dramas are essentially
the serialized novels of the Information Age,

After a walk through the neighborhood with my host
and his dog, bearded, masked, muscular, restless at leash,
quivering to pursue scents unknown,
to contribute his own,
to leap upon the legs of neighbors and strangers,
after a dinner bounty of fowl and greens peppered with
enthusiasm and generosity and just the right seasoning,
after the gift savored of aging-bachelor-fellowship,
with its web of brisk melancholy and circumvented yen,

After waiting for the bus, imbibing the double dose of the smoke
of smokers in the shelter, whose smoke did not seem second-hand
but rather first-hand, omnipresent, inescapable, despite the outdoors,
despite my edging away from the bus sign and the stop altogether,
and the smoke of traffic pollution, reflecting upon the sludge
clotting our rivers, the deserts born of once meadows,
the water rising to erase once beaches and islands and …
the lung cancer of a colleague who never smoked and
never was around smokers (as I was at that moment),

After traversing the barrenness of the Sunday night train platform,
as if the throngs of tomorrow could not possibly be summoned,
I looked out the train window, past the spectre of my transience,
onto the river, surely best not swum,
a river that did not surge, was never called mighty,
although agreements epic were said to have been negotiated alongside,

a river, whose modesty was belied by the grandeur of the monuments
gleaming whitely below the violet of this night, a wraith of water
whose banks were chosen for the site of the capital of vast ambition,

And I was reminded of the fragility of connection in the fray of the natural
world, of the will needed to mend that world, and of the staccato
of progress in the realms of nature and medicine (and natural medicine),
and I was hopeful that a convergence of science and supplication would
yield miracles on the macro and micro levels, and I was grateful,
even in the accretion of smoke in skin, for the grandeur of this political
experiment, some of whose signposts were just now passing, for the green
yet remaining, for the candy of costume narrative, and for the asylum
awaiting me in my brief sequence of rooms only just beyond.

Before Dusk in the Herb Garden

There is a time of day
when the herb garden green of my bathroom is not folly,
when the remarks of friends—
of one: that she could never apply make-up against this backdrop,
of another: that these walls evoke pea soup,
and of another: that it needs to be changed immediately
for there should be a law with a heavy fine levied against walls this color
and of a gentle yet another: that the color is really not so terrible—
do not sting and do not linger in soap or skin
but are only periodically examined from within a desk drawer

There is a time of day
when the herb garden green of my bathroom is not folly,
when I recall the excitement of color selection
in the big box store, the whirling/weaving of elements on the wheel/loom,
my need to bring garden indoors,
to feel myself nude daily in green,
my wish to heighten the green of the Yiddish poster announcing sports
tournaments of muscular Jews who would not long thereafter likely
have been felled into mass graves in the forests of Poland or elsewhere,
and I am reminded of the forest's ability to conceal and to restore

There is a time of day
when the herb garden green of my bathroom is not folly,
when the beige-ness that preceded it does not at all beckon
when the privilege of ownership of home, however small it may be,
of finally having entered adulthood and of having made it
as defined in a land of plenty (for some),
is laced, but not doused, with ambivalence,
for yes the bathroom is quite small, and the floor tiles so worn,
and the bathtub surround and the sink countertop are so very plastic
and it's really the bank that owns all of this anyway

There is a time of day
when the herb garden green of my bathroom is not folly,
when the rays of the setting sun beam through the window

and transform the walls into panels of green gold brightness
and I am walking whitely after bath
into a grove of leaf and quiet
whispered to by Jewish athletes doing chin-ups in the forests of Poland
and all that I have known to be folly final and irrevocable is mere mistake,
and perhaps minor at that, or perhaps simply steps on a path pebbly,
to be embraced in the light of ebbing day.

Birds of the Southern North

In memory of Beyle Schaechter-Gottesman, 1920-2013

In this small town,
where my second language has a seat at the university table,
in a land where I've only just discovered it is an official minority language,
I wander through drizzle and rain and seldom-sun
to marvel along winding cobbled streets,
at the architectural interplay between one-story cottages,
ornate nineteenth-century edifices of higher learning,
and modern structures,
with their economical lines and shrewd details,
for which the region became so known in the center of the last century.

As I wander, I hear the words of the language of the land
whose meanings are unknown to me,
even if the sounds and cadences are not entirely unfamiliar
after years of watching the films of the cinema master
and even if many of its words are similar
to words in my second language
which I note while watching subtitled television and
listening to the rain chime
against the skylights in the sloped ceilings
at night after wandering.

There's little opportunity on this brief trip for absorption,
let alone mastery. Instead, the sounds cascade over me
in a singsong of long vowels and yellow.
When my friend and host asks me if I detect the difference
between this language and that of the nearby land,
I gawp at her in disbelief.
My fourth and fifth languages require diving into dictionaries
and limit my attendance at the art cinema.
And yet I am regularly assured that I can get by with my first language.
And yet I am unsettled.

At once cerrated and clear, the call of crows
reverberates across green,
between august historical buildings,
and directly into my musings on land and language.

Their famed aggression nestles in the tangle of my not-quite-apartness.
Never have I heard their call with such clarity and with such force.
Never have I encountered them in such great number, in apparent ubiquity.
What's the word for a group of them? *Murder?* No surprise there.
And their size! Gleaming blackly and hugely,
they thrive in this cold and damp and north.

Even at dusk and into night, as my wanderings continue,
I hear their call. Seemingly, they never tire.
And I remember a line from the Yiddish poet only recently departed:
*"Di shvartse vorones zey vern nisht mid/*the black crows, they never tire"
And I think of her own dedication to her art through
wanderings far more geographically epic than mine,
and of the intimacy and wisdom of her carefully hewn lines,
in poem and song and drawing.
And I remember the writers' circle gatherings at which she presided,
offering encouragement and a firm hand extended to us all.

And I remember the first summer of my second-language instruction,
as I wandered the almost equally unfamiliar streets of Brooklyn,
the thrill of immersion in this new-old language,
playing the newly released cassette of her songs on my portable player,
a device long since jettisoned.
Where is that cassette player now?
The song of the indefatigable crows will forever be connected
to my initiation into the formal study of my second language,
the poet the conductor
and the crows the accompaniment in cacophonic symphony.

And I pause in my wandering, turn to face, not the music, but the noise.
All that I thought I knew turned out to be perhaps not so.
The brutality in which I was forged did not break me.
That which I assumed required burial could be disinterred,
if initially into candlelight and shadow.
My col/lapse into shards of memory is no cause for dismay.
These many years later, the past is available for investigation.
I trek through soundscapes adjacent to the terra of the terror familiar,
stopping occasionally to fondle the scabs. The poet smiles upon me;
the crows of then and now accompany me into the disappearance of dusk.

Lund, Sweden, October 2014/Tishre 5775

קיין מאָל האָב איך ניט פֿריער געהאָרעט זייער רוף מיט אַזאַ קלאָרקייט און מיט אַזאַ כּוח.
קיין מאָל האָב איך זיך ניט פֿריער באַגעגנט אַזויפֿיל פֿון זיי, כּלומרשטיק אומעטום.
ווי וואָלט מען אָנגערופֿן אַ טשאַטע פֿון זיי? מערדער? ניט קיין חידוש דאָס.
און זייער גרייס! גלאַנצנדיק שוואַרץ און גרויס,
געדימען זיי אינעם קעלט און פֿײַכטקייט און צפֿון.

אַפֿילו צו בין־השמשות און אַריֵן אין דער נאַכט, בשעת איך וואַנדער וויַטער,
הער איך זייער רוף. כּלומרשטיק ווערן זיי ניט מיד.
און כ'געדענק אַ שורה פֿון דער ייִדישער פֿאָעטעסע נאָר וואָס אוועק אין דער אייביקייט:
"די שוואַרצע וואָראָנעס זיי ווערן ניט מיד."
און איך טראַכט וועגן איר איבערגעגעבנקייט צו איר קונסט דורך
וואַנדערונגען אַ סך מער געאָגראַפֿיש־עפֿיש ווי מײַנע,
און וועגן דער אינטימקייט און חכמה פֿון אירע שורות געטעסעט אַזוי פֿאָרזיכטיק,
אין ליד און געזאַנג און צײַכענונג.
און כ'געדענק די שרײַבבקריבוזן מיט וועלכע זי האָט אָנגעפֿירט,
און אונדז אַלעמען געמוטיקט און אויסגעשטרעקט אַ פֿעסטע האַנט.

און כ'געדענק דעם זומער דעם מיַן צווייטער־שפּראַך־אינסטרוקציע,
בשעת איך האָב געוואַנדערט איבער די כּמעט־פּונקט־אַלכע־פֿרעמדע גאַסן פֿון ברוקלין,
דעם תּענוג פֿון טבֿילה אין דער נײַער־אַלטער שפּראַך,
שפּילנדיק די נײַע־אַרויסגעגעבענע טאַשמע פֿון אירע לידער אויף מײַן פֿאָרטאַטיוון שפּילער,
אַ מיטל לאַנג שוין אַרויסגעוואָרפֿן.
ווו איז דער מאַשין איצט?
דאָס געזאַנג פֿון די וואָראַנעס־וואָס־ווערן־ניט־מיד־ וועט אייביק זײַן פֿאַרבונדן
מיט מײַן ארינפֿיר אינעם פֿאָרמעלן לימוד פֿון מײַן צווייטער שפּראַך,
די פֿאָעטעסע די רעזשיסאָרקע
און די וואָראַנעס די באַגלייטונג אין קאַקאָפֿאָנישער סימפֿאָניע.

און כ'שטעל זיך אָפּ אין מײַן וואַנדערן, דרײַ זיך צו קוקן פּנים־אל־פּנים ניט צו דער מוזיק,
נאָר צום טומל.
אַלץ וואָס ס'האָט זיך מיר געדאַכט אַז איך וווייס איז צום סוף אפֿשר געווען אַדערש.
די ברוטאַלקייט וואָס האָט מיך אויסגעשמידט האָט מיך ניט צעבראָכן.
דאָס וואָס כ'האָב אָנגעמונען אַז עס פֿאָדערט קבֿורה האָט מען געקענט אויסגראָבן,
כאַטש בײַם אָנהייב אין ליכט און שאָטן.
צוליב מײַן אײַנברערעכן זיך אין זכרון־פֿראַגמענטן דאַרף איז זיך ניט מיאש זײַן.
נאָך די אַלע יאָרן קען מען נאָך אַלץ אויספֿאָרשן דעם עבֿר.
איך גיי אַדורך קלאַנגשאַפֿטן שכינותדיקע צו דער ערד פֿונעם באַקאַנטן שרעק,
און איך שטעל זיך אָפּ פֿון צײַט צו צײַט צו צערטלען די סטרופֿעס. די פֿאָעטעסע שמייכלט אויף מיר;
די וואָראַנעס פֿון אַמאָל און הײַנט באַגלייטן מיך אין דער פֿאַרשווינדונגען פֿון בין־
השמשות אַרײַן.

לונד, שוועדן, אָקטאָבער 2014/תּשרי תּשע״ח

פֿײגל פֿונעם דרומדיקן צפֿון

בײלע שעכטער-גאָטעסמאַנען, 1920-2013, אין אָנדענק

אינעם קליינעם שטעטל,
ווו מײן צווייטע שפּראַך האָט אַ זיצאָרט בײם אוניווערסיטעט-טיש,
אין אַ לאַנד ווו איך האָב ערשט אַנטדעקט אַז זי איז אַן אָפֿיציעלע מינדערהײט-שפּראַך,
וואַנדער איך אַדורך רעגנדל און רעגן און זעלטן-זון
צו גאָפֿן מיט וואונדער פֿאַזע שלענגלדיקע ברוקירטע גאַסן,
אויפֿן אַרכיטעקטישן אויסבעט צווישן אײן-שטאָקיקע הײזקעס,
אָרנאַמענטירטע נײנצן-יאָרהונדערטע געבײען פֿון העכערע-לימודים,
און מאָדערנע סטרוקטורן,
מיט זייערע עקאָנאָמישע ליניעס און חריפֿותדיקע פּרטים,
צוליב וועלכן דער ראַיאָן איז אַזוי באַרימט געוואָרן אין מיטן פֿאַרגאַנגענעם יאָרהונדערט.

בשעת מײן וואַנדערן הער איך די ווערטער פֿון אַ לאַנד
וואָס זייערע באַטײטן זײנען מיר אומבאַקאַנט,
כאָטש די קלאַנגען און ריטמען זײנען מיר ניט אין גאַנצן אומבאַקאַנט
נאָך יאָרן קוקן אויף די פֿילמען פֿונעם קינאָ-מײסטער
און אַפֿילו ווען אַ סך פֿון די ווערטער זײנען ענלעך
צו ווערטער אין מײן צווייטע שפּראַך
וואָס איך אַנטדעק בשעת איך קוק אויף טעלעוויזיע מיט אונטערגעקעפּלעך און
צוהערנדיק צום רעגן וואָס קלינגט
אויף די דאַכפֿאָרטקעס אין די משופּעדיקע סטעליעס
בײ נאַכט נאָך מײן וואַנדערן.

פֿאַראַן ווייניק געלעגנהײט בשעת דער קורצער נסיעה דאָס אַלץ אײנצוזאַפּן,
שוין אָפּגערעדט פֿון מײסטערשאַפֿט. אַנשטאָט דעם פֿאַלן די קלאַנגען אַראָפּ אויף מיר
אין אַ טראַאַלאַיע לאַנגע וואָקאַלן און געלע.
ווען מײן חבֿרטע און גאַסטגעבערין פֿרעגט מיך צי איך קען אונטערשיידן
צווישן דער שפּראַך דאָ און דער פֿונעם שכנישן לאַנד,
קוק איך איר אָן מיט ניט-גלויבן.
מײנע פּערטע און פֿינפֿטע שפּראַקן באַדאַרף איך שטאַרק זוכן אין ווערטערביכער אַרײן
און איך בין באַגרענעצט אין מײן בײזיצן אין דער קונסט-קינאָ.
און דאָ פֿאַרזיכערערט מען מיך שטענדיק אַז איך קען אויסקומען מיט מײן ערשטער שפּראַך.
און דאָך בין איך ניט-רוייק.

מיט אײן קלאָפּ געצאַקנט און קלאָר קלינגט אָפּ דער רוף פֿון וואָראָנעס
אַריבער דעם גרין,
צווישן דערהויבענע היסטאָרישע בנינים,
און אין מײנע הירהורים אויף לאַנד און שפּראַך גלײך אַרײן.
זייער באַרימטע אַגרעסיע ליגט אײנגענונרעט אינעם פּלאַנטער פֿון מײן ניט-אין-
גאַנצן-באַזונדערקײט.

The Intruder Overhead

There is a tiger in the attic.
Its paws thud across floorboards that groan in protest.
The glass in the windows rattles in its frames;
the amulets bequeathed to you by Gran rustle in their blankets.
Directed by Blume with the crown of black braids and the bisque face,
your dolls, the Lorelei of long ago, trill lullabies in tinny unison
in an effort to temper the thunder of the tiger's march.
For all the sturdiness of its foundation, for all the grace of its lines
envisioned by your grandfather and built with the men of the village,
this house can surely not long withstand the tiger's insistence.
Mother, I tremble in tempo with the foundation, and I am afraid.

There is a tiger in the attic.
Foam drips from its whiskers.
Its black stripes have magnified a thousand fold and
transformed into tentacles tight around my skull.
The orange negative space between the stripes
has scorched the barbed wire looming over our once-sturdy shelter.
Hacking into the secrets of our paltry pantry,
its blue eyes penetrate the abyss of my dread.
The gloom you've polished into gleam
buckles under the clarity of its knowing.
Mother, I gaze upon the inferno of its determination, and I am afraid.

There is a tiger in the attic.
Sounds emanate from between the ridges of its jagged throat.
First there is mewling,
as if its younger, domesticated alter-ego is exploring hay in a barn.
Then, with greater certainty, there is displeasure expressed,
deceptive in the abruptness of its brevity.
Finally, a roar relentless batters the Lady Baltimore cakes that cool
on the marble sideboard. The lemon frosting must still be applied.
The tranquility you've embroidered these many decades
dangles rent beneath the transoms.
Mother, I absorb the staccato of these proclamations, and I am afraid.

There is a tiger in the attic.
And yes we know of its loss of lair,
the power of those in pursuit of its skin's warmth, its fur's glory.
And thus we are the latest witnesses to the tiger's fate,
to the vulnerability belied by rippling flanks and cerulean depths,
to the scarlet streak of the macaw's plumage against the jungle wall so
evident in the tiger's yowl. And yes we believe in co-existence, as we've
discussed while the milk bottles rattled in their crates on the threshold.
What shall become of this house?
How shall we fortify the fragility of home?
Mother, I pose these questions, and I am afraid.

And so I stagger up the twisted staircase to the attic to face the feline
whose plight has grown no less dire while I have been dithering.
A candle's flame shielded by glass flickers in my hand;
its shadows gyrate over the wainscoting and the veins in the ceiling.
The tiger pauses in its pacing. In that respite, in that intake of breath,
I search for the fuel for the transformation of fear, so carefully cultivated
these many years, for the determination to continue on towards a clearing
in which the tiger and I lie entwined under a midnight moon.
I imagine the tiger's crouch as I approach.
The lace of your encouragement flutters as a veil before me, Mother,
and a shawl all around.

פֿאַראַן אַ טיגער אויפֿן ב וידעם.

און מיר ווייסן יאָ פֿון זײַן אָנווערן די נאָרע,

דער מאַכט פֿון די וואָס לויפֿן אים נאָך צוליב דער הויטס וואַרמקייט, דער פעלצס גלאַריע.

און דערפֿאַר זײַנען מיר פֿון די נײַסטע עדות צום טיגערס גורל,

צו דער שפּיווועקדיקייט באַהאַלטן אונטער מוסקולעזע פֿלאַנקען און בלויע טיפֿעגישן,

צום רויטן פֿאַס פֿונעם מאַקאַוס פֿעדערן אַטנקוגען דער דזשאַנגל-וואַנט אַזוי

קעגטיק אינעם טיגערס יאָמער. און מיר גלייבן יאָ אין אין מיטזײַן, ווי מיר האָבן

דיסקוטירט בשעת די מילך-פֿלעשלעך האָבן געשאַקלט אין די קאַסטנס אויפֿן שוועל.

וואָס וועט ווערן פֿונעם הויז?

ווי זאָלן מיר באַפֿעסטיקן די ברעכיקייט פֿון אַ היים?

מאַמע, איך שטעל צו די פֿראַגעס, און איך האָב מורא.

און דערפֿאַר שטאַמפֿער איך ארויף די פֿאַרדרייטע טרעפּ אויפֿן בוידעם אַרײַן צו קוקן פּנים-אל-פּנים

אויף דעם קאַטער וועמענס מצב איז געוואָרן ניט ווינציקער גרוייליק בשעת מײַן וואָקלעניש.

אַ ליכט פֿאַרשטעלט פֿון גלאָז צאַנקט אין דער האַנט;

די שאָטנס טאַנצן איבער די ווענט און די אָדערן פֿון סטעליע.

דער טיגער שטעלט זיך אָף אינעם אַרומשפּאַנען. אין אָט דער הפֿסקה, אין אָט דער ניט-אָטעמען,

זוך איך ברענווואַרג אויף צו פֿאַרוואַנדלען מורא וואָס איך האָב אַזוי פֿאַרזיכטיק קולטיוויוירט

די אַלע יאָרן, אויף דער פֿעסטקייט וווּטער צו גיין אויף צו קומען צו אַ פֿאַליאַנע

אין וואָס דער טיגער און איך ליגן צונויפֿגעפֿלאָכטן אונטער אַ האַלבע-הוילער-לבֿנה.

איך שטעל זיך פֿאַר דעם טיגערס הויערן בשעת מײַן דערנענטערן זיך.

דער פֿאַזומענט פֿון דײַן דערמוטיקונג פֿלאַטערט פֿאַראויס ווי אַ שלייער, מאַמע,

און ווי אַ שאַל אַרום אומעטום.

דער אַריַינדרינגער אויבן

פֿאַראַן אַ טיגער אויפֿן בוידעם.
זײנע לאַפּעס לישען איבער די דיל-ברעטן וואָס קרעכצן אין פּראַטעסט.
די גלאָז אין די פֿענצטער שאָקלט זיך אין די ראַמען;
די קמיעות דיר אָפּגעזאָגט פֿון דער באַבען שאַרכן אין די קאָלדרעס.
אָנגעפֿירט פֿון בלומען מיט דער קרוין שװאָרצע צעף אונעם פֿאַרצעליַינעם פּנים,
זינגען דײנע ליאַלקעס, די לאַרעליַיען פֿון אַמאָל, װיגלידער אין צינענדיקן אוניסאָן
כדי צו פֿאַרװיַיכערן דעם דונער פֿונעם טיגערס מאַרש.
ניט געקוקט אויף דער קרעפּקעניש פֿונעם פֿונדאַמענט, ניט געקוקט אויף דער גראַציעזקייט
פֿון די ליניעס
אויסגעטראַכט פֿון דיַין זיַידע און געבויט פֿון די מענער אין דאָרף,
קען דאָס הויז זיכער ניט בײַשטיין דעם טיגערס צושטייַיקייט.
מאַמע, איך ציטער אין טעמפּאָ מיטן פֿונדאַמענט, און איך האָב מורא.

פֿאַראַן אַ טיגער אויפֿן בוידעם.
שום טריפֿט פֿון די װאָנצעלעך.
די שװאָרצע פּאַסיקעס האָבן זיך אַ טויזנט מאָל פֿאַרגרעסערט און
זיך פֿאַרװאַנדלט אויף טאָפּערלעך ענג אַרום מיַין שאַרבן.
דאָס אָראַנזשענע נעגאַטיװע געשפּרייט צווישן די פּאַסיקעס
האָבן פֿאַרשרפֿהעט דעם "שטעכיק-דראַט" וואָס לויערט איבער אונדזער אַמאָליקן קרעפּקן אָפּדאַך.
אַריַינהאַקנדיק אין די סודות פֿון אונדזערע מאַגערער שפּיזזאַרניע,
דרינגען זײנע בלויע אויגן אַריַין אין תּהום פֿון מיַין אימה.
די מראָקע וואָס דו האָסט געפֿוצט אויף גלאָנציק
פֿאַרשטאָלט זיך אונטער דער קלאָרקייט פֿון זײַן וויַיסן.
מאַמע, איך קוק אָן אויפֿן גיהנום פֿון זײַן פֿעסטקייט, און איך האָב מורא.

פֿאַראַן אַ טיגער אויפֿן בוידעם.
קלאָנגען קומען אַרויס פֿון צווישן די קאַמען פֿון זײַן געצאַקנטן גאָרגל.
צוערשט איז דאָ מיַאַוקען,
ווי זײַן יינגערער, איַינגעשטובעװיקט אַלטער-זיך פֿאָרשט אויס הי אין אַ שיַער.
דערנאָך מיט גרויס זיכערקייט דרוקט זיך אויס אומצופֿרידנקייט,
אָפֿנאַריש אין דער פּלוצעמדיקייט פֿון קורצקייט.
צום סוף צעשלאָגט אַן אומרחמנותדיקער ברום די "ליַידי באַלטימאר" קוכנס וואָס קילן זיך אָפּ
אויף דער מאַרמאַרנער קרעדענץ. די לימענע באַצוקערונג מוז מען נאָך אַלץ צולייַיגן.
די שלווה וואָס דו האָסט די אַלע יאָרצענדלינגער אויסגעגאַנייט
העַנגט, צעריסן אונטער די באַלקן-פֿענצטער.
מאַמע, איך זאַפּ איַין די סטאַקאַטו פֿון די פּראָקלאַמאַציעס, און איך האָב מורא.

Exit Stage Left

And although there is surely more to tell, it is nearly time to take
our leave of the daffodil and his friends you've encountered
earlier in his *Education*. But before we depart, let's pause at the door,
now ajar, of his conservatory. You may be shocked at his appearance
for no longer is he the tank he had for so many years been.
The daffodil has turned in the tank—
rusty, creaking, and excruciatingly painful to maintain—
and is back again to being a daffodil,
slender of stem and (somewhat) bright of bulb.
You will want to know the keys to this return.

And let it suffice to say here that such keys
included touch of the body that was determined yet gentle,
excavating far below topsoil into accretions
of history and closet, unsettling and ushering them into letting-go
and needles on meridian points
and food for fuel and not for the hoarding of horror
and dialogue wide-ranging and yet guided within boundaries.
For the daffodil ventured into worlds alternative where he was not rushed
through a waiting room crowded and where his accounts of terror
were not not met with pity or revulsion or distance.

And though his glance is rarely returned on the street or elsewhere
and though his knight has not yet arrived at his threshold
and though his bed is still unshared
except for a stuffed piglet gifted him by a beau of long ago
and though the hair of his head and body is turning fast to snow
and though he wears no dresses,
there is light in his fingers and a foxtrot in his step and stardust scattered
throughout his song. And the daffodil does read of books widely
and luxuriate in words read and written,
and does find dignity in the measure of days and nights quietly spent so.

And see now the daffodil well off the center stage, before a mirror,
with only a dressing table lamp as illumination.
He is not hunched over, nor writhing in the pain that used to sear

his body. As you depart his tale, or these chapters of it,
see him in this stillness, devoid of frame or adornment of any kind. But
wait! Here is the daffodil rising to greet you, to give thanks for having
remained to learn of his *Education* penned in these (very) long poems.
And so you leave for now, and the daffodil will be not long behind.
For the stage is not his natural habitat, and back to the land by the lake
to flutter and dance in the breeze shall the daffodil soon go.

Acknowledgments

I am grateful to the editors of the following publications in which these poems, sometimes in different form, appeared or are scheduled to appear.

- *Apeiron Review* (February 2016): "Before Dusk in the Herb Garden" and "Movement, in Black and White"

- *Beltway Poetry Quarterly* (Spring 2016): "First Fruit (and Aftermath)" Between: New Gay Poetry (Chelsea Station Editions, 2013): "To the Boathouse"

- *Dead Snakes* (December 1, 2014): "Dialogues in Transit," "Dreams of Declamation: an Invitation," and "Love in the Reign of Raining Rockets"

- *Foliate Oak Literary Magazine* (February 2016): "The Intruder Overhead" and "Return of the Repressed"

- *Forverts* (September 2016) and *Penshaft: New Yiddish Writing* (September 23, 2016): "Birds of the Southern North" (Yiddish)

- *The Hamilton Stone Review* (October 2014): "Alley Apparition (Without Pierogis)"

- *Hill Rag* (September 2014): "Orphan's Dowry"

- *Jewrotica*: "From Night to Night," (October 22, 2014) "In Blue Moonlight," (December 31, 2014) and "Portrait of a Predecessor" (December 3, 2014)

- *The Lake*: "Fellowship Prize(d)" (July 2014) and "Temperance Movements" (August 2014)

- *Liberation: New Works on Freedom From Internationally Renowned Poets* (Beacon Press, 2015): "Refugees from Little League"

- *Masque & Spectacle* (March 1, 2015): "1:00 A.M. Beneath Bronze Arches"

- *miller's pond poetry magazine* (Winter 2014): "The Problem of Cacophony"

- *The Ofi Press Magazine* (October 2014): "Clarissa's Convocation of Muses"

THE EDUCATION OF A DAFFODIL

- *Petals in the Pan* (Kind of a Hurricane Press, 2015): "A Knight Shining Without Armor"

- *Pyrokinection* (July 2, 2014): "Radio Nights in Candyland"

- *Queens College Journal of Jewish Studies* (Spring 2014): "Cautionary Tale" and "Silent No More, or, Notes on Melodrama Re-Visited"

- *A Touch of Saccharine* (Kind of a Hurricane Press, 2014): "Candy Tattoo" and "Diabetic's Fantasia"

- *The Tower Journal* (Spring-Summer 2015): "Midnight in the Garden of Gridiron," "Musings (Made Up) of Melanie," and "On a Given Sunday"

- *The Wax Paper* (forthcoming): "Revolutionaries on Holiday"

- *Wild Violet Magazine* (January 4, 2015): "The Introvert Who (Almost) Ran for Town Council"

- *Writing Raw* (August 2015): "Birds of the Southern North (English)," "Concerts by the Sea," and "In Bed with the Widow Empress"

- "Fellowship Prize(d)" was nominated for a Pushcart Prize by John Murphy, editor of *The Lake*

- "A Knight Shining, Without Armor" was included in *Storm Cycle*, Kind of a Hurricane Press's "Best of" anthology for 2014

I am indebted to the Virginia Center for the Creative Arts (VCCA) for awarding me a residency, during which this book was conceived and structured and many of these poems were written.

I am grateful to Elena Djima of Hadassa Word Press for her belief in this project and for guiding the manuscript through the publication process. I thank Carmen Calatayud, Deborah Leipziger, Joseph Ross, Leslie Contreras Schwartz, and Matthew Thorburn for their generous blurbs.

Sheva Zucker proofread the Yiddish version of "Cautionary Tale," "Refugees from Little League," "Dreams of Declamation: an Invitation," and "Birds of the Southern North" as well as the title of the book. Miriam Koral proofread the Yiddish version of "First Fruit (and Aftermath)" and "The Intruder Overhead." Their feedback greatly improved my work, and I am grateful to them for so generously sharing their expertise.

I am grateful to the following individuals for support: Angelika Bammer, Anne Becker, Andrew W.M. Beierle, Zackary Sholem Berger, Susana H. Case, Ellen

Cassedy, Cindy Casey, Jim Feldman and Natalie Wexler, Krysia Fisher, Ken Giese, Pearl Gluck, James Hafner, Elizabeth Heaney, Miriam Isaacs, Howard Jaffe, Kate James and Scott Fontenot, Julia Spicher Kasdorf, Cecile Esther Kuznitz, Laura Levitt, Jeff Mann, Erin McGonigle, Yankl Salant, Paul Edward Schaper, Jeffrey Shandler, Barbara Buckman Strasko, Laura Van Prooyen, and T. Michael Womack.

Elizabeth Goll Lerner, Jennifer Ray, Mark Rush, Emily Siegel, and Phil Tavolacci offered essential guidance and wisdom. In ways direct and indirect, their insights and praxis helped usher this book into being. My beacons are they all.

Printed by Books on Demand GmbH, Norderstedt / Germany